Trying to Fly

ANNIE TRY

First published in Great Britain in 2017

Instant Apostle
The Barn
1 Watford House Lane
Watford
Herts
WD17 1BJ

British Library Cataloguing-in-Publication Data

A catalogue record for this book is available from the British Library.

This book and all other Instant Apostle books are available from Instant Apostle:

Website: www.instantapostle.com
E-mail: info@instantapostle.com

ISBN 978-1-909728-61-5

Printed in Great Britain

For my children:
Steph, James, Tim, Susie and Beth,
whose clamour for 'made-up' stories helped mould me as
a writer.

1

Summer, 1956

Before that day, I used to love summer Sundays. Except for those when I had to wear my best starched-linen dress and cover my head, sitting still and silent on hard pews in the Quaker meeting. I knew I should meditate, but I wasn't really sure what that meant, so I usually thanked God for Mummy and Daddy and then counted the spiders I could see rebuilding their webs. Mummy and the other Quaker ladies cleaned the meeting room on Saturday, which is why Sunday was the spiders' building day. The webs were all shiny where they stretched across the window – these were the castles of the princess spiders.

I loved building, too, so on the special outing Sundays when we didn't go to meetings I took my bucket and spade, swinging them as I hurried ahead down the cliff path and steps to the beach. Mummy always shouted at me, 'Jenny, keep away from the edge – don't go over the fence – mind how you go on these steps.' Or sometimes, 'Jenny, wait!'

On this particular Sunday, Aunt Judy and Uncle Peter had come and it was Aunt Judy's turn to bring the picnic. She carried it in a large wicker hamper, and Uncle Peter carried a Thermos full of tea for all the grown-ups and a big bottle of cherry pop, mostly for me.

Daddy was with us for a change, so instead of running in front of everyone else I rode high on Daddy's shoulders, looking down on Mummy and Aunt Judy. I could smell the Brylcreem in Daddy's black hair and feel his thick neck as I clenched it between my legs. Daddy ran along the cliff path with me up there – holding my arms out, as we became a biplane. I was really flying, swooping up and down. Then Mummy was calling, 'Don't go too near the edge.'

Daddy swung me down from his shoulders and held my hand as we jumped on each of the forty-three steps and ran onto the pebbled beach to stop near a high wooden groyne.

When we reached the soft sand, I couldn't wait to begin to dig. Aunt Judy arrived and shooed me out of the way as she spread out her beach blanket and established our patch for the day. I pulled off my sandals and socks and buried my toes in the warmth of the sand. I was too hot in my jumper so Mummy helped me to strip down to my polka dot shorts and vest before she disappeared under her huge kaftan, which she saved for the seaside. After a lot of wriggling she emerged in her new royal blue shiny swimsuit. She looked like a model, except her brown curly hair was all blowing about. Daddy was already in his swimming shorts and he pulled her down the beach towards the sea. Mummy shouted back, 'Judy, keep an eye on Jenny, would you?'

They knew I'd prefer to collect shells, dig and build. I always did. I found some damp sand near some rock pools as far away from Aunt Judy as she'd let me go, and began making a hole. Today it would be a special pool – I was going to call it 'The Sweetheart Lake' – with shells in lines round the edge and an island in the middle with my flag in it. I scooped out the soft sand, watching the hole fill with water as I dug deeper and deeper. I added more water, collecting a few tiny crabs from the rock pools by mistake. The cockle shells looked white and crinkly as I lined them up along the edge with a few grey mussels every now and again. The sand here was cool and wet. I paddled in my sweetheart lake feeling the sand swirl around my feet, then sat on the edge with my feet in the water – my legs bent high over the shells lest I spoil their order.

My back was to the noise of the sea, so from where I sat I could see the sand, then the shingle that stretched back to the cliff. There weren't many people near us on the beach that day. I watched some bigger children climb up the steps near the small beach café with its assortment of battered tables and rusty chairs stretching out onto the pebbled beach. Hundreds of gulls swooped over the roof of the café and down onto people's leftover chips and pasties. A bird rose far up into the air; my eyes followed it as it dipped and soared. It was then that I saw the man.

Outlined against the blue cloudless sky, he was high on the edge of the cliff, arms outstretched like the wings of an eagle. He stood there, tall and straight. Then he dropped his arms to his sides and turned, making his way towards the fence, the same fence Mummy had said I should never climb over. I put my hand up to shade my eyes from the sun and looked for him along the clifftop again. He was coming back, now, walking towards the cliff edge.

I ran as fast as I could to our picnic spot.

Uncle Peter was the nearest adult, but he was lying on a towel with a newspaper over his eyes. It looked like he was asleep, so I jumped over his legs to get to my aunty.

'Aunt Judy, Aunt Judy – there's a man on the cliff and he's the wrong side of the fence.' I was gasping for breath as I tugged at Aunt Judy's sleeve. She was busy, carefully laying out the picnic on a blue gingham cloth. Aunt Judy always liked her picnic to look good, so she had arranged our egg and cress sandwiches, neatly triangled, into a pretty pattern on the plate in the middle of the cloth, with five blue napkins and matching cruet.

'You're getting sand on the sandwiches, dear. Move back from the cloth.'

'But, Aunt Judy – the man has climbed over the fence.'

'I'm sure he has good reason, dear, now go back and finish digging your big hole. Don't watch him if it bothers you.'

I trailed my spade in the sand as I made my way back to my sweetheart lake. I didn't like Aunt Judy calling it a hole, so I picked up a few more pretty shells on the way to decorate it and make it look even more special.

But I couldn't help looking up. I could see the man was still there, right on the edge, but even as I shielded my eyes he did something extraordinary. I couldn't see his face properly, but I could see what he did with his arm. He pointed to his head, then his tummy, then his shoulder and the other shoulder. He put his arms out again and stepped forward. There was light all around him. He must be a holy man ready to fly. I would see someone flying, like Peter Pan! I held my breath while he stood there on the very,

very edge. He just balanced. I watched him, waiting. I couldn't even hear the gulls any more. Was he going to take off in the sky? Up to heaven? I heard my heart pounding as he looked up, his arms still stretched out. He stayed there for ages. Then he calmly stepped forward. I saw his foot as he walked off the cliff. I wished and wished he would fly.

I gasped as he fell.

There was a loud thump as he landed. I could see a limp arm hanging over the edge of the café roof. It looked as if it moved but then it flopped. Why didn't he fly? He shouldn't have gone near the edge of the cliff if he couldn't fly. I knew this was desperately important so I rushed back to tell the grown-ups.

'Aunt Judy, the man jumped and he can't move now!'

'Did he, dear? Well, I never, what will you think of next? Mind that sand – run down and see if your mother and father have finished their swim, would you? Oh, and wake up Uncle Peter – there's a love.'

Mummy and Daddy were on their way up the beach – Mummy wrapped up in her big stripy towel and Daddy looking blue and goose-bumpy. Mummy had found me a wonderful shiny shell that glistened with little rainbows when I turned it. I pulled her over to see my sweetheart lake and to put the shell in the special place in the centre of the top V of the heart.

Mummy didn't call my pool a 'hole', but admired the way I had set the shells in rows and made the shape. The island had dissolved into the water, but it still looked like a wonderful lake. Mummy picked me up, wrapping both of us in the huge towel so that I was pressed against her wet swimsuit, my arms round her neck with my face buried in salty, sandy strands of her hair. She smelled of seaweed and saltiness and my mother all at once. I hugged her tight.

'A man was trying to fly,' I said in her cold ear, among the soggy hair.

'Let's make you fly,' said my mother, pulling me round in front of her, then grabbing my hands to swing me free from her body and round, and around, and around – the stripy towel flying off her towards the gingham cloth.

'Mind the picnic,' called Aunt Judy. Mother and I fell laughing together.

'Don't fuss so, Judy. We'll have crunchy sandwiches like we always do!'

Wrapped in her bright kaftan, my mother settled beside me and we were ready to eat the feast Aunt Judy had prepared. The sandwiches had been joined by little pork pies, her own home-made pickle, cheese and crackers, some fairy cakes and, only for me, a packet of crisps with little twists of salt in royal blue shiny paper that matched Mummy's new swimsuit. Aunt Judy knew that crisps were my absolute most favourite things to eat on a picnic.

'Sandwiches first, remember, Jenny,' said Aunt Judy. She poured me a drink of cherry pop and I felt that usual comfy Sunday outing feeling of everyone being friends while we ate. Even Uncle Peter joined in when we were eating, making jokes about getting in a pickle or being crackers. But no one was as good as my daddy when we were eating together. I forgot all about the holy man on the cliff as Daddy tucked his napkin into the neck of his shirt, carefully checked his hands were clear of sand, including under his nails, then turned all his attention on me. He cut cheese bricks to make a tower on my plate, and then he changed his mind and arranged them with a triangular sandwich into a house with half a cracker for a door. I was his princess and he was my attendant for this picnic on the beach.

I leant against my mother and half-listened to her and Aunt Judy as they gossiped about mutual friends and people we could hardly see on the television that Daddy had made when it was the Queen's coronation. Aunt Judy always talked as if she knew those people on the television as her friends. 'I agree with Fanny when she says food should be presented as something really exciting, so that people have their appetites whetted.'

I didn't know why people had to have wet appetites, but maybe it was when they felt dribbly before a meal. A gull came near us with his eye on the sandwiches, and Daddy clapped and waved his hairy arms to make him go away. Those greedy birds would try to eat anything. It made me think of the gulls picking up the chips near the café.

I remembered the man trying to fly. Why couldn't he do it? Maybe he should have bent his knees to push himself up in the air. Or maybe he should have practised first. I could see the top of the café from here, but the arm was not hanging over the edge any more. Mummy had said if you fell off a cliff you would die. Someone else was up on the roof now, sometimes standing up and sometimes bending over something – I knew the person must be looking at the man.

There was the noise of a Sea Rescue helicopter overhead and we all stood up, trying to see what was happening. Daddy spotted a police car which had arrived up on the cliff road. This was soon followed by an ambulance, drowning the call of the gulls with its clanging bell.

Uncle Peter ran up the shingle towards the café. I wanted to go too, but was told, 'This isn't for little girls; eat your crisps.' I hadn't finished my sandwiches but, checking Aunt Judy wasn't watching, I opened up the crisps, unscrewed the blue paper and shook the lumpy salt into the bag. I didn't mind the lumps: it made some crisps ordinary and others all sharp and tangy. If I closed my eyes I could make it like a surprise dip, with sometimes very salty or not salty crisps. They were delicious.

The grown-ups were all trying to talk to each other with whispers and nods. Maybe they had secrets to talk about. I took my crisps and went to eat them by my lake.

I couldn't hear the helicopter any more and no bells were ringing, so with my eyes closed I could hear the screeching seagulls and the sea again and taste the crisps. Now everything felt like it should on the beach on Sunday outing days. I ate the crisps very slowly, trying not to crackle the packet to break the spell.

When I could find no more crisps by touch, I opened my eyes and saw that Uncle Peter was back with Mummy, Daddy and Aunt Judy. He was moving his arms about, pointing at the café and telling them something. It looked exciting. I ran over and the grown-ups went quiet. I thought I was in trouble for going off to eat my crisps. I hung my head. Aunt Judy put her hand on my shoulder and spoke quietly, 'Come on child, stop drooping about. Help me pack up the picnic.'

'I haven't finished,' I said, picking up my plate with its half-eaten house of cheese and sandwich.

She took it from me. 'We'll all finish our picnic at home, dear. Hurry along now.'

Mummy struggled to lift me high up on the breakwater, my legs dangling far above the beach. She gave my feet a rough, stinging rub with her towel, before my socks and sandals were put back on. She turned to roll the wet towel and I pulled my legs up, placing my feet on the top of the breakwater post. The next one along was even higher so I walked along the ledge in between them, balancing with my arms out, then I tried standing up straight. I wobbled a bit before I got my balance. I was very high. I felt very powerful. I was much, much higher than I had been on Daddy's shoulders. I stretched out my arms again as I looked at the blue sky, the gulls and the shingle below me. Then I did that special sign I'd seen the man do – touching my head, my tummy, my shoulders. I felt excited and very strong. I reached out my arms even wider – with the whole of my being I so wanted to fly. I bent my knees a little, then with all my energy I willed myself to soar through the air.

I pushed myself off towards the sky.

2

The beach looks the same, fifty years on. I am standing with my back to the sea, confronting my nightmare. Many, many nightmares, in fact. As you know, Mike, they have plagued me ever since. I now wish I had taken your advice and brought someone here with me. I appreciated your suggestion that you should come but, you know me, the thought of being on a beach with my psychologist made me squirm with embarrassment. Sorry I couldn't tell you that in the session. But I will try to record my thoughts and everything on the little recording machine you lent me when we were working on my first excursions from the house. Right now, I'm breathing a bit fast so I need to come up with one of those positive statements you always suggest. Here goes: *I, Jenny Drake, recovering agoraphobic, have made it here on my own – I am 'master of my own healing'* (as you would say, ignoring the fact that I'm female).

I am kicking pebbles and shells – I am now picking up a large cockle and thinking of the sweetheart lake. I dare not look up to the cliff, not yet, even though I have just walked along the neat but sandy boarding of the well-fenced cliff path. Now I am here, I am not sure what I should do. What would you suggest, Mike, if you were with me? You'd probably tell me to think about physical sensations – connect, maybe, with my surroundings. Well, I can feel the sand has found its way into my sandals by the grittiness between my toes. I can hear the black-headed gulls making a huge racket. I can feel the warm sun on my face. Part of me wants to be six again – wants to build a lake. But I am afraid out here on the beach, more afraid now than I was as a child when my imagination saved me from what was unravelling before my eyes. I was powerless to stop it. I told myself the man was trying to fly. I tried to tell my aunt, then my mother, but no one would listen.

Oh, blast – now I've thought about the man. My body is beginning to shake as my eyes feel drawn towards the cliff. I'm not ready. I must breathe slowly, calm myself, count downwards from ten, pray, let my feelings subside. Okay – done that; now I will turn to the sea and remember my mother in that shiny blue swimwear.

Even that's a mistake, Mike; my eyes are filling with tears. I miss her so much. While she was alive I more or less coped. I'll stand looking out to sea and try to concentrate on remembering what happened after the event, the bit I haven't told you about.

I broke my leg when I jumped off the groyne. I have forgotten the intensity of the pain now, but I do remember my leg looked wonky and I felt as if the world was turning around me. Mummy and Aunt Judy put the picnic blanket over me while Uncle Peter rushed up to the café to get an ambulance to come for me. They took me off to the hospital for an X-ray. It was a bad fracture, in two places.

When my mother told the doctors all that had happened on the beach that afternoon, they thought I had been trying to kill myself. Was I? You asked me that, and I couldn't answer. I don't know to this day, but I do know that for a few heady moments I wanted to fly – no, more than that, I *yearned* to fly. The power of it took me over; I was so sure of myself – limitless. But, like anyone else, I fell to the ground and broke.

When I had been back home for a week or two, in our little house where Daddy used to say you couldn't swing a cat, a psychiatrist came to see me. My mother called him a 'feelings doctor'. He had grey hair which looked oily; he had little round spectacles and a dark stripy suit. No one asked him to sit down, but he came and perched on the other end of the couch where I was sitting with my leg propped up. I was embarrassed because I thought he could see my knickers from there, so I pulled my cardy off and stuffed it between my legs. He laughed and called to my mother to fetch a blanket or something to 'cover her modesty'. I feel the heat rising to my face when I think about it even now. Why couldn't the silly man sit on another chair? Every time he moved, the hard white plaster rubbed on my thigh and my leg hurt more than ever.

He asked me lots of easy questions, like my name, my school, my best friend. I was still cross, so I gave him grumpy answers. Then it got nasty – with some 'why?' questions. I clamped my lips together and refused to answer – except silently in my thoughts.

'Why did you say the man was trying to fly, Jenny?'

I was thinking: *Maybe he was. I thought he was. You weren't there.*

'Why didn't you tell someone in your family about the man, Jenny?'

I did, I did, I did. No one listened to me.

'Why did you jump, Jenny? Did you want to die?'

I don't know, I don't know, I don't know. Leave me alone.

I remember sniffing loudly to alert my mother, who pulled herself upright in her chair and crossed her arms before saying, 'You're upsetting her.'

'Sometimes, Mrs Drake, we need to work through the upset to help children like Jenny.'

'My leg hurts, Mummy,' I whispered through my tears.

My mother came and knelt beside me. I felt the soothing stroke of her fingers through my hair. 'Couldn't you leave it until she's in less pain?'

The feelings doctor peered at me with his small probing eyes. I was now sobbing extra hard. I hid my face in the warmth of my mother. I hated him. I was never, never, never going to talk to him again. Come to think of it, he's probably the reason I took so long to find help when I couldn't get out of the house.

My mother agreed to contact him when my leg was better. Somehow she never did get round to it. She knew how stubborn I could be and didn't ever mention it again. I wonder now what my life would have been like if I had talked to someone earlier on – not that psychiatrist, but a children's nurse, or someone like you. Maybe I wouldn't have had those nightmares. Perhaps I would have been a confident, outgoing person.

3

I've sat down on the beach, now, Mike, still looking out to sea. There are several other people staring at the waves while they talk into mobile phones, so I don't stand out. It's very peaceful, looking at the colours of the sea with the glint of the sun highlighting the gently rolling waves. While I look in this direction, I feel quite serene. I can hear children running around behind me, shouting to each other, and there are a couple of teenage girls splashing each other in the sea, just over to my right. They are giggling and bobbing up and down, scooping handfuls of water over each other before running high-legged through the shallow waves. The smaller one's bright orange, sodden T-shirt is clinging to her body and her rolled-up jeans look black with the wetness. She has water running through her curly hair, reminding me of the feel of my mother's wet, salty strands.

If I turn round, I know I shall have to look at the cliff. But if I do, I shall probably panic. So I will have to steel myself to keep looking at the sand and the shingle. I know – I'll take my sandals off. That will make me concentrate on my feet to avoid any sharp pebbles or shells.

One more deep breath…

I'm going to leave the beach now.

Notes made back at Jasmine Cottage, Bideford
7.30pm, Tuesday 24th

If you've listened to the tape, Mike, you'll know I stopped recording when I turned to walk up the beach. Not intentionally. I dropped the recorder into my bag while I took off my shoes. I was going to take it out and resume my running commentary, but what happened next put it out of my mind.

When I turned round, the first thing I saw was a little girl of about six digging a pool. It made me stop in my tracks. But I calmed myself down (deep breathing and positive thoughts!) and convinced myself I was not going mad. The child was wearing a bikini, not at all like the swimsuit I had as a child, so I was able to rationalise the scene and remind myself it was 2006, not 1956. Her family were near the breakwater – maybe the same one my family had sat by all those years ago. They were nothing like my family. There was a plastic striped windbreak round them, a baby in a buggy crying loudly, and they were eating chips out of polystyrene trays. The smell of the chips wafted over to me and I remembered I hadn't eaten any lunch.

I was making my way past the family, with their little girl digging on my right. I concentrated on looking at the sand and even picked up a few shells. Then I reached the shingle and it was too painful on the feet to walk without sandals. I sat down to put them on. The seagulls were all round me now – probably attracted by the chips. Then the little girl began to shriek and I realised that she too had a portion of chips. I charged back along the beach waving my arms to frighten away the birds – the child stopped shrieking as the birds flew off. I slumped down on the sand. My heart was thumping.

The little girl stared at me, then turned and ran over to her family, who had not stirred themselves to help her. I noticed her pool was circled with cockle shells.

All the family were looking at me so, as soon as I could, I stood up, gave them a wave and turned to go back up the beach. I forgot to look down. My eyes followed a gull as it soared high up in the air. On the top of the cliff stood a man.

That's when the panic took over. I half-ran, half-stumbled up to the open door of the café. I had to get indoors. I pushed through the tables to the furthest corner and, turning my back on curious eyes, I put my head in my hands. I was shaking all over. I couldn't control the noise of my breathing as I gulped for air. All I could hear was my own gasping breath. Then a child started to cry.

I heard the scrape of the metal chair on the tiled floor as someone sat opposite me. A man's stubby, tanned hand pushed a box of tissues under my bowed head. 'You all right, love?' The voice had a soft Devon accent.

I tried to nod, but felt too dizzy. When I spoke, my voice wobbled. 'There's someone on the edge of the cliff.'

The owner of the voice rushed off. I felt so dizzy I couldn't move my head. It felt like ages before he came back. His voice was soothing, careful.

'It's okay – there's no one there. It was probably only someone trying to get a better view or take a photo. You've had a shock, I reckon. You take your time. I'll fetch you a cup of tea and maybe you can tell me what happened.'

I knew I was making a fool of myself, so that made me feel worse. But people were now chatting behind me, and it all sounded quite ordinary. I was able to practise my slower breathing. The buzzing in my ears died down and I began to take control. I was less shaky by the time the hand reappeared in front of me holding a mug of tea.

'I've put sugar in it. For shock.'

I cupped the warm blue and white mug in my hands, trying to steady myself to sip it. It was very hot and oversweet and sickly, but concentrating on trying to drink helped me stop trembling. In front of me was a broad expanse of white overall with small green embroidered lettering, 'The Beachfarer'.

'Sorry,' I said. 'Panic attack.'

'Any particular reason?'

'It's a long story. You probably wouldn't understand.'

'Try me. I'm Jim. I work here. We're not very busy today, and Chrissie over there will cope with any more customers, so I've plenty of time.'

I glanced up and saw a young girl in a black skirt with a white pinny. She was sauntering over towards a far table where a group of young men were greeting each other loudly as they pushed back their chairs to sit down.

I looked at Jim properly for the first time. He had crinkly greyish hair and smile lines from the corners of his dark eyes. He appeared to be in his sixties. His face was chubby and tanned. An outdoor face. A face you could trust. He was smiling, encouraging me to talk.

So I did. I started with when I was six. I told him about the outings on Sundays, about the lake and the picnic. Then I hesitated.

'So what happened on that day to upset you so much now?'

I looked at him. He was leaning forward and seemed genuinely concerned. It took me a few minutes to say. My hands were clenching and unclenching on my lap under the table. I took control of them and placed them together, trying to draw strength from a silent prayer. Jim sat quietly, patiently, waiting for me to tell him. Then I blurted it out. 'A man jumped off the cliff and killed himself.'

There was a sharp intake of breath from Jim. Then a pause before he said so softly that I could barely hear, 'I remember that day.'

4

Before Jim could offer an explanation, Chrissie came over. 'Sorry, Jim, do we have any sausage rolls left?'

'Not warm ones. But the oven is on; I'll come and see to putting some more in. How many do we need?'

Chrissie looked back towards the table of noisy lads. 'They all said they wanted one, so five.'

Jim turned to me. 'Excuse me, I'll be back in a minute. Don't go anywhere.'

I sat and waited for him. Questions were pouring through my mind. *What did he remember? Was he on the beach? Did he see the ambulance?*

It seemed to take him ages to sort out a few sausage rolls, but then he came back and sat down opposite me again. 'Do you want me to tell you what I saw?'

I nodded; I did want to know, yet I didn't.

'I was twelve,' said Jim. 'My father owned the café and we all helped – my two brothers, my sister and myself. I liked doing it; they didn't. On that day my mum was there too, because we reckoned that what with the weather being so good we would do some brisk business. In fact, it was a bit of a slow day. You didn't come into the café at all, did you?'

23

'No, it was Sunday. We were Quakers: we never bought anything on a Sunday,' I said, apologetically.

'Ah, well, you should have changed your day to Saturday – Dad was in the process of building the business up and he was already getting a good reputation for his fish and chips. I was out cleaning the tables and swatting gulls when I heard the bump – the man landing on the roof – you know.'

I swallowed hard. I did know. Images crowded into my mind. The man silhouetted against the sky. The sun behind him. His outstretched arms, the take-off, the moment when he didn't fly. I put my hands on the table ready to stand up and make for the door. I began to shake.

'You all right?' he asked, gently touching one of my hands.

I nodded, trying to turn my thoughts to the tables outside the café. I couldn't remember having seen anyone wiping them, but it was quite a way off and I was watching the man on the cliff.

'I ran back into the café to find my dad, who was busy frying. He kept saying things like, "What sort of thump? A seagull falling? Someone throwing something from the cliff?" It took me a while to get him to take it seriously, then he left the frying to my mum and we went through the back and put up the ladder to the roof hatch together. Dad went through first. He was chatting to me, telling me it wouldn't have been much, but he jolly well hoped the cliff wasn't crumbling. He turned and stuck his head through the hatch. I heard him gasp, then scramble onto the roof.'

Jim paused and took a sip of his tea. I didn't dare ask what happened next. He glanced at me and started to talk again, more slowly. 'My heart was going nineteen to the dozen when I scrambled up the ladder and through the hatch. My father was leaning over a man. There was blood by the man's head. I couldn't go closer; I was frozen like a statue. My dad rolled him on his back and started to push on his chest. He shouted at me to go and get help.'

I nodded. I remembered the limp arm over the edge of the roof. I had seen it move – in my nightmares it waved and I did nothing. I was shouting but I couldn't make people listen. I was forever running but never getting there. Sometimes I was swooping, flying, falling, dropping into darkness.

My voice cracked as I spoke. 'Was it you who called the ambulance?'

'Yes, and we called the police. They sent a Sea Rescue helicopter, for some reason.'

'I saw the helicopter.'

We sat quietly for a while. I was trying to imagine Jim as a boy of twelve – still a child – seeing the body, calling the ambulance, having to grow up. We both started to talk at once:

'Did you…'

'Were you…'

'After you,' he said.

'I was wondering if you knew who he was, or anything about him.'

'He'd been in the café a few times, but I didn't know where he came from, or who he was. He was always on his own, except for once, when he was with someone much younger than him. Why do you want to know?'

'I don't know. I was only a kid, and I thought he was...'
I stopped myself from saying what I thought he was doing,
and shrugged. Some things you think as a child make no
sense as an adult.

'I was angry,' said Jim, 'really angry. Dad was working
so hard to make the business a success, and then we had to
shut up the café for the next two weeks while it was all
taped off and swarming with police. We have no idea what
that was about, even now. Mum was going spare because
with no café, there was no income. By the second week we
had to go to my aunt's for meals. Mum never heard the last
of that. And to crown it all the weather was glorious, the
two best weeks of the season.'

'That's strange – I wonder what the police were looking
for.'

'Plenty of mystery surrounding that chap, that's for
sure.'

He sighed. I felt uncomfortable that I'd made him think
about all this, even though I now felt slightly more
detached from it than I ever had before. What had been my
private nightmare and had felt like my fault for all these
years now only claimed my partial ownership. Silently, I
thanked God for this meeting. I stood up.

'I think I'm okay to brave the world now. Thanks for
your help.'

'Are you sure? Tell you what, I'll let Chrissie know, and
then I'll see you to your car.'

So he did. He walked with me up the cliff path,
chattering all the time about the weather, the number of
tourists this year, the renovations he wanted to do to the

café. Each time I glanced at him or made a comment, his face crinkled as he smiled. I didn't even feel faint.

We reached the car and he offered me his hand. 'You didn't tell me your name,'

'I'm Jenny – Jenny Drake.'

'Pleased to meet you, Jenny Drake. I'm Jim Tyler.'

We shook hands solemnly. He was looking straight into my face, but I couldn't hold his gaze. I pulled my hand away and put my key in the door of the hired car.

As I turned it, he said, 'Come back again, Jenny, won't you? You still haven't tasted our fish and chips. Come to the café first, if you like, and we can have a bit of a walk on the beach.'

I slid into the driver's seat, slipping the key into the ignition. I could feel my face reddening. It was bad enough not being able to cope on the beach without some stranger offering to walk with me.

'Thanks, but you've helped me enough already.'

Jim looked puzzled at the tone of my voice. 'I'm sorry – I didn't mean... Look, I've got the café's email address here. Contact me, if you want, or at least let me know when you're next visiting.'

I took the page he'd torn off the notepad taken from his apron pocket. It was a little greasy round the edges – obviously paper more suited to taking down a customer's order. I felt heat still in my face and neck, but I glanced at the note briefly before dropping it onto the passenger seat and muttering, 'Thank you.'

I started the engine and began to reverse the car out of the parking space. Jim grinned and did a little thumbs-up sign. I found myself smiling, and drove out onto the road without even thinking of looking back along the top of the cliff.

5

A few days later, I was back in London. On Monday, I was early for my appointment with Mike. I always left enough time for panics on the way, but I had made it with none that morning. Feeling more confident than usual, I took my seat in the waiting area of the Department of Clinical Psychology and studied the posters on the noticeboard – nothing added since the previous week except a note to say that the Head of Department was on holiday and please address urgent enquiries to Dr Mike Lewis. I briefly wondered about Mike, my psychologist, being second-in-command for what seemed to be quite a large department. He was certainly an efficient psychologist, having helped me this far, but otherwise he seemed so disordered.

I told myself it was none of my business, and took out my notebook to begin to write some more notes for the session. Well, that's what I intended to do, but I found myself writing, *Why did the police spend two weeks in the café? Or was it only on the café roof? What were they looking for? Who was the man? Did he have a history of mental illness? What was it all about?*

By the time Mike had seen his previous client out, I was totally immersed in thinking about the mystery man. I had scribbled a whole page full of ideas, from the ludicrous *He was a British agent* to the rather more likely *They were trying to establish his identity.* Mike's voice made me jump. 'Hi Jenny, are you ready to see me?'

I pushed my notebook back into my handbag and followed Mike into the untidy clutter of his room. This was a familiar place; I had been a weekly visitor for most of the past three months, having gradually worked up to being able to make the journey from Kennington. Prior to that he had visited me at home, helping me to leave the house until I could reach the Tube station. I was no longer petrified of being here, sitting in his tatty armchair, feeling sorry for his dying potted plant, wondering why his wife never took his corduroy jacket to the cleaners or helped him find a tie that matched his shirt. I was so much better that we had agreed to stretch out my sessions to fortnightly.

'How was your journey today, Jenny?' Mike could be very predictable with his opening questions – usually about the journey, or my health. For once, I was able to be positive with my reply.

'No panics. Not one. Not even in the Underground while I was waiting.'

'That's a first, isn't it?'

'Yes, it definitely is.'

Mike smiled. I felt very smug as I smiled back. 'A Cheshire Cat moment,' as my mother would have said.

'So is your new-found confidence anything to do with your little jaunt to the beach, do you think?'

'It didn't feel like a little jaunt; some of it was terrifying.'

'I know. I'm sorry, I didn't mean to make light of what was in fact a great act of courage. I've listened to the tape and read the notes you sent. I think you did extremely well,

30

even though you went against my advice and went on your own.'

'Sorry about that – it was simply that being in Devon, the opportunity was there.'

'No harm done. You survived it, and from what you've written it seems that it has helped you become more detached from what happened when you were a kid. Do you still feel like that?'

'Yes – and no.'

Mike gave me one of his quizzical looks and stroked his unruly red beard.

I tried to explain. 'Well, in some ways I still can't get it all out of my head. But I've only had two nightmares since I saw you last, and even those weren't so bad. I haven't had the falling one at all. The thing is, I'm sort of...'

I searched for the right word – Mike waited patiently, his head slightly to one side. I avoided his gaze while I searched for the right word. *Intrigued* would be about right, but seemed too dramatic. I toned it down.

'... *curious*. I've spent so long trying not to let it dominate my thoughts, and now I *want* to think about it. I want to know about the man who jumped. Why he was there, in that particular bay, at that particular time; who he was; why the police spent so long in the café – all of it, what did it mean?'

Mike was grinning. 'You have certainly worked something through here. Do you think it was your conversation with the café owner – Jim – that has helped you take a different view of things?'

'I think so. He certainly said or did something that helped me out of the panic. He's the only person who's done that apart from my mother – and you, of course. But out there, in the real world…'

'As opposed to this fictional one, do you mean?' asked Mike, waving his hand around his room to include the dirty coffee cups on the top of the filing cabinet and the leaning, disordered pile of files on his desk.

I smiled. 'Yes, as opposed to the safety of this room. In the real world no one has come to help me sort out a panic before.'

'Has anyone ever had the opportunity? You've usually bolted back home, or into the car.'

'I suppose that's true. This was the first time I was too far away from the car.'

'Also, you had to go up to the cliff to reach it. That might have proved quite a deterrent under the circumstances.'

I imagined myself climbing the cliff path to the car park on my own. I shuddered, even though I was only thinking about it. Mike was right. 'I couldn't have got that far – I was desperate to be indoors.'

'It will take time to overcome the last vestiges of the agoraphobia. And if you will go charging off doing things we've only discussed in theory, you are going to find yourself in new situations where you have to find instant solutions, like rushing into a café.'

'It was the only thing I could do at the time.'

'I realise that and it worked out well – you found you were capable of more than you knew. But getting to Devon in the first place was a major achievement in itself. How did that come about? Did you stay with your aunt?'

I replied to the second question first. 'Yes. Aunt Judy was having a weekend in London and did something to her hip. She rang me on the Wednesday to ask if I could drive her back to Devon because she thought she'd cope better in a car rather than the train. I couldn't very well tell her that I usually panicked before I got as far as Reading.'

'So you felt cornered, then?'

'Definitely. You don't say "No" to Aunt Judy! I had no option but to go for it. I was pretty much all right on the way down; she kept up a constant stream of small talk which served as a good distraction.'

'What about on the way back?'

'It was hard, but I coped. I kept to the B roads, mostly, and had plenty of breaks. I did panic in Salisbury. I was going to walk into the services to get some lunch to eat back in the car.'

I paused, remembering. I could feel my body becoming tense. Mike distracted me by asking, 'Did you have to stay hungry?'

What a practical question! I managed a slightly false laugh and felt myself relax a little. 'Not quite. I had taken a packet of crisps and an apple with me, so I ate those and carried on.'

Mike nodded and stroked his beard. 'Okay, so what have you learned from the whole experience?'

I hated it when Mike asked me that sort of question. I thought for a while and threw out a few phrases at random, hoping one of them would be along the right lines.

'To control my breathing? To find out about things to make them less frightening? That what happened to me is only part of the picture? That I can do things I didn't think I could do? That praying helps me become more calm?

That there are some people out there who will help me when I panic?'

Mike smiled and held up his hand. 'Whoa, there,' he said. 'That's a lot to talk about!'

'Sorry!'

'No, don't apologise. All those answers are absolutely correct, but there are some things you've missed out.'

'What are they?'

'I think you have learned to ignore your psychologist! I am most impressed that you decided when you'd go to the beach and worked out how you'd cope when you were there. As far as I'm concerned, those are the most important things you have done here.'

I didn't know what to say to that. I shrugged.

Mike raised his eyebrows and, with his head on one side, he stroked his beard again, then asked, 'Well, Jenny, what opportunities do you have before you now? And what will you decide to do next?'

6

I knew perfectly well what I wanted to do next. But I didn't tell Mike. For the past few days I had been unable to stop thinking about the whole beach experience. Not the original one, with the man trying to fly, but the day the previous week when I had panicked and fled into the café. Odd images had kept flooding into my mind – they were steadily pushing out those frightening, falling scenes, even the memory of leaping off the breakwater. These were different, comforting images. A logo saying 'The Beachfarer', a pair of stubby brown hands, hot, sweet tea in a white and blue striped china mug. Here was someone else with a different memory – perhaps an even more horrific memory. Someone ready to talk about it and really understand.

So what I needed to do next was to ring or email Jim. I wasn't terribly sure whether my email account was up and running. My neighbour's son, Sam, had set it up before Mum died when I had wanted to use it to find an online course and update my training, but I hadn't got round to it. In my youth, when I found it difficult – but not impossible – to leave the house, I forced myself to attend college and train as a librarian. I built up my confidence and over the years I worked in several libraries, only leaving my job as chief librarian when Mother became ill. No computers then, of course, but nowadays every library had them, or so I'd been told. I had yet to discover for myself. The work on my agoraphobia that I undertook with Mike had got me as far as shops and museums with him or his assistant. I could probably cope with a library on my own. Maybe that was something I would attempt after emailing Jim.

My computer was in the upstairs box room, covered in dust with all the leads unplugged. I remembered moving it out of the dining room when it became Mother's bedroom in the later stages of her illness. It took me some time to clean everything up and match all the plugs with the shaped sockets on the back of the computer. When I switched on, nothing happened, and it was another twenty minutes before I realised that the monitor was switched off. Then all sprang into life, and I consulted the notes that Sam had left me to find my way into cyberspace.

Most of the afternoon was taken up with setting up a new email account, because I couldn't remember the password to get into the old one. It was with a feeling of immense satisfaction that I eventually started to compose an email to send to Jim. How should I begin? 'Dear Jim' seemed too formal for an email. I started writing.

I was very pleased that I could have a few goes at it, because everything I typed seemed overenthusiastic to begin with. At one stage I wrote about how intrigued I was by the mystery man and that I was very eager to know more about him. I nearly sent this one, before I noticed it could have looked as if I were writing about Jim.

Two cups of coffee and many attempts later, I decided to scrap all my previous efforts and go for short and sweet.

Jim
Good to meet you. Thanks for your help last week. If you know anything else about the mystery cliff man, I'd be interested to hear.
Best wishes
Jenny

I wondered whether even this was a bit too friendly, but I clicked 'send' anyway.

Too late now to try to make my way to the library – I wasn't sure about opening times, in any case. I felt strangely deflated. The satisfaction of sending the email was overshadowed by the feeling that anyone else would have dashed it off in a few minutes. I was useless. What had I done with my life? What was the point in getting interested in anything? What was the point in constantly driving myself to do things and go places? I was in my mid-fifties and agoraphobic. No, correction: 'recovering agoraphobic'. Desperately trying to undo the slide into a fear of everything that enveloped me after my mother's death. Even my faith, which had jogged along as a comforter, had dispersed. I prayed, but felt my prayers were going nowhere – why would God worry about someone like me? Most of the time I felt very, very alone.

I made myself go to find a meal-for-one from the freezer and poured myself another coffee while cardboard lasagne whirled round in the microwave. I didn't have much of an appetite. Eating had become little more than part of my routine – but that was better than when Mother was dying and I kept forgetting about feeding myself. Yet once again, it was another meal on my own, sat in front of the television, watching something in which I had absolutely no interest.

To save myself the disappointment of no reply, I didn't check my computer until Wednesday. When I did I was amazed to find fourteen unread messages. Being a novice emailer, I was unprepared for the deluge of advertising, mostly for tablets to sort out rather masculine problems. But among all these strange senders with their peculiar names were two emails from Jim. I clicked on the one nearest the top of the list before I realised I was reading them in the wrong order.

> *PS I forgot to say, if you let me have your phone number I can ring you if it is the right chap and I find out anything more. God bless, Jim.*

Who's 'the right chap', I wondered as I fiddled around trying to close one message and open the next. Eventually I managed it:

> *Hi Jenny*
> *I'm really glad to hear from you. I have grilled my poor father and he has rummaged through his memory cells to tell me what he can. The man who jumped was Henry Standish and Dad thinks he was a policeman who had taken early retirement. Dad said that people who knew Standish did not believe he would commit suicide. The rumour went round that he was secretly working on something that would have huge implications at government level.*

Dad thinks Gloria Standish, his wife, became very ill and went to a nursing home in Totnes. He doesn't know if she came out again. She's probably dead by now – unless she's lived to be over 90. Dad remembered his son was Frederick – he came across him, perhaps thirty years ago, in the Bell and Whistle in Flyncombe. He recognised Dad and they chatted a little about what happened. Dad had the impression that the Bell and Whistle was Freddie's local. He thinks he told him he was an accountant.

I have looked up his name in the phone book – there is still an F. Standish, so I'll ring later and see if he's the right chap. He's not listed in the Yellow Pages under accountants.

Look what you've started – I've managed not to think much about this for all those years, and now I've turned into some sort of investigator!

See you soon, I hope!

Jim

I didn't take ages to work out a reply – I went for it:

Hi Jim

This is all really interesting. Please let me know the next instalment. Here's my number: 01238 365721. Is there anything I can follow up from here?

Jenny

7

Next day, as I was brushing my hair in the morning, it occurred to me that I was now corresponding with a man who was really a complete stranger. Well, I suppose I had met him, but I only had his word for who he was, and he might be making up that he had been there when the man had jumped. I surveyed my image in the glass, trying to be objective. Would he lie to get to know me? I suppose I still had high cheekbones and my face wasn't too wrinkled, but there were an awful lot of grey hairs speckled among the 'strawberry blonde', as my mother used to call this odd orangey colour. My mother's regular home hairdresser, Sheila, had carried on coming only for me after Mum died, so my hair usually looked neat and fairly sleek, although its texture had harshened as the grey sneaked in. The shoulder-length bob was probably a bit dated; I made a mental note to ask Sheila if a more modern style would suit me. Perhaps layered and shorter?

I took extra care putting on moisturiser and lipstick and plucking a few stray brows. Not that I was seeing anyone that day, unless I did manage to go to the library, but simply to see what I could make of myself with a little effort. I tried some brown eye shadow. It looked awful, but the merest hint of green looked okay, with a little brown/black mascara to prove I really did have lashes. They are almost invisible against my skin without the extra darkening.

I scrutinised the result. Not too bad. I could do with something to make my hair look glossy, and maybe a bit of blusher – I looked deathly pale. Not sure anyone would lie for me, especially not someone as nice as Jim.

I found myself gazing, astonished, in the mirror. This was maybe the moment when I let myself accept the thought that it wasn't only the mystery man I was interested in; it was Jim as well. What nonsense – an old maid like me! Anyway, he was probably married with a host of adult children and even a few grandchildren.

Nevertheless, the first thing I did that day was look on the computer. No new message from Jim, although 'Vladmak' offered me 'New X-site-mEnt'. I blotted Vladmak out with a smart click on delete. I then did the same to all the other advertisers, having remembered Sam warning me not to open anything that might be suspicious. It felt quite powerful and very contemporary to be organising my own inbox. But with nothing new in it, I couldn't help feeling a little disappointed. I checked that my reply to Jim had been sent – and, yes, it was there with the other sent item, my first email to him.

I reread his email with its separate postscript. I thought about the way he signed himself off – 'God bless, Jim'. I wondered if he went to church. My mother and I used to go to the Baptist chapel when we moved here, but agoraphobia had put an end to that. People used to visit from the chapel, but then gave up after my mother died, although they sent the occasional note saying they had missed me and hoped I'd be free to come to chapel soon. I didn't tell anyone my life was closing in around me until I never went anywhere.

I went and made myself a cup of tea. I took my teapot off the shelf, then put it back, thinking one cup would do. As I stirred the teabag round in a flowery mug, I reasoned that not everyone checked their computer several times a day, so I may not receive a reply for a while. I took a single custard cream out of the Clarice Cliff biscuit barrel my mother had found in a junk shop thirty years ago. The biscuit was soft and stale – one packet lasted too long to stay fresh. Despite all those advertisers who had emailed clamouring for my attention, I felt extraordinarily lonely.

It was Friday before I heard from Jim. I had spent a miserable couple of days trying to make myself attempt the trip to the library, but I kept reasoning that Jim might call so I ought to be here. Mike had warned me about this, the fact that my mind would always find a reason for staying in rather than pushing myself to go somewhere, but this was different. There was someone who had said he'd ring, but he hadn't said when that would happen.

At first when the phone rang, I thought it was on the television. It was so rare that I received phone calls in the evening that by the time I realised, I rushed to the phone to pick it up. My heart hammered as I said, 'Hello.' A deep voice with a gentle Devon burr answered me. I found myself smiling as I replied, 'Oh, hello, Jim. It's really good of you to ring.'

What a stupid thing to say! I sounded so pathetic. Luckily, Jim didn't seem to notice.

'I've met Freddie Standish, Jenny, so I thought you'd like to know how I got on.'

'Yes, I would.'

My nervousness was making me talk nonsense. Couldn't I have thought of something a little more interesting to say?

'Well, he's exactly as you'd expect an accountant to be, really. Sort of well-groomed and authoritative. I told him what I remembered about his father's death and that I'd met someone who, as a small child, had witnessed it too. He asked me a few questions to check me out before he said anything much. But then he told me he definitely doesn't believe his father committed suicide. Freddie remembers his dad as being full of excitement about setting up his new business. That's all he would talk about.'

I was struggling to calm my nerves and think of something to say. Between deep breaths I managed, 'That's interesting. Um... What about his father's marriage?'

'Freddie thinks it's unlikely there were difficulties there. He remembers his father as a very open man, and he and his mum were "soppy together". He doubted his dad would have had another woman. They didn't seem to have any hidden secrets. Mind you, it's difficult to know whether he would have had a clear idea of his father.'

'How old would he have been?' I asked.

'He's not much older than me, so he would have been in his mid to late teens then.'

'So was there anything he could tell you that was more, sort of, I don't know, more hard facts?'

'Well, there is one interesting point. Freddie could remember the police searching his father's study. He thought it very strange at the time, when they were saying he had committed suicide. He started to chat with one of the young constables about what they were looking for, and the policeman had said, "Oh, various papers and bits that might be of interest, you know, to do with what he was working on," when his sergeant had turned and said, quite firmly, "A suicide note, young man. We're looking for a suicide note." He thought it was most peculiar that the constable didn't seem to know. Freddie was into song-writing at the time and he wrote down the whole conversation as material for a song about his father's death.'

'Did he write the song?' I asked, immediately wishing I hadn't. 'Sorry, silly question.'

Jim laughed softly. 'I don't know. I didn't think to ask him. But I did ask him if he still had his notes and he said he'd have a look. I also asked him about the time before his father died and he said that in the morning he was meant to be studying for exams, but wasn't really doing much. So his dad set him some work and told him he was going to check what he'd revised when he got back.'

'That rather sounds like he intended to return. Did he say where he was going?'

'Yes, he was meeting someone in Flyncombe. Freddie said, "Maybe in this very pub," and we both looked at each other and turned towards the barman, who looked about ninety. Freddie asked him when he started work there, and unfortunately it was only twenty years ago, so no joy there.'

'Maybe he knows someone who was around then who could say if Mr Standish did meet someone in the pub. Did he eat a meal there, do we know?'

'Probably not, because he had told Freddie's mother he would be home by six to cook the roast in the evening. Apparently he loved cooking and often cooked on a Sunday if he didn't go to church.'

'Where did he go to church? Was that in Flyncombe?'

'No, I asked Freddie that. Henry went to the local Catholic church. He was quite into his faith – which Freddie says is another reason why his dad would never have committed suicide. Apparently it's a sin.'

'Is there anyone apart from the coroner who thinks it was suicide?'

'Freddie has never been able to find anyone among his father's friends or his relatives who thought he would take his life. Not a soul. In fact, they think it was out of character for him to have been walking along a clifftop when he could have been home with his family. His best friend apparently said that even to be there he must have been very ill, or hallucinating.'

I thought about the man, standing on the cliff edge, crossing himself. He didn't look ill; he looked powerful. I felt myself begin to shake.

'Jenny, Jenny, are you still there?'

I gulped. I tried to concentrate on the man in the pub talking to Jim. 'Sorry, Jim. I'm trying to remember things.'

'Well, don't think about it too much. It gets into your mind. I've taken years to get over it.'

I nearly told Jim then. So few people understand that something that frightens you so much as a child can affect your whole life.

'I know. I try not to think about it. So back to you talking to Henry's son, if there wasn't a meeting in the pub, where else might it have been?'

'Well, I know of at least one other pub and a small hotel. Then there are some tea rooms in the high street, but I'm not sure they are open on a Sunday. Nowhere used to be, really, apart from pubs.'

'I suppose you've ruled out churches?'

'Now, there's an interesting point. I hadn't thought about that. I suppose the time would be about right. Do Catholics have services at eleven? Freddie said he left home at about ten-thirty. There you go, Jenny, that's something that you can find out. A list of pubs and hotels in Flyncombe in the 1950s and the time of the services in the Catholic church. '

'And maybe the other churches and chapels, too. After all, the person he met may not have been a Catholic.'

'Good point. Why don't you ring or email me when you've done that? Meanwhile, I'll be following up anything else I can think of here. Perhaps the local papers – I expect they'll be archived in the library. What do you think?'

'Yes, great idea.'

'Oh, and one more thing. Gloria Standish is alive and living in the old family home in Devon.'

'She must be quite old. Is she well enough to speak to us?'

'Sorry, I forgot to ask. I'd best go now, Jenny. My son, my brother-in-law and his wife are waiting. They're taking me out for my birthday.'

'Oh, happy birthday. I hope you have a great evening. Bye.'

'Bye, Jenny, speak to you soon.'

I put the phone back and wandered into the kitchen. Apart from feeling nervous, I'd felt so good talking to Jim right up until he had to go. There was a lot to think about, but all I could concentrate on was Jim. I felt unaccountably uncomfortable as I realised that if he had a son, that meant he was married. I could picture him with his wife on his arm, and a younger version of him at his side, laughing as they all got into the car, with Jim joking about the strange, panicky, middle-aged woman who was interested in something that happened half a century ago.

I ran the water into the kettle. As I did so, I decided that whatever I found out, I would not contact Jim again. I'd wait for him to get back to me.

8

Over the next few days I spent many hours on my computer. I was still on dial-up, so I dreaded to think what the phone bill would be like. Even with my limited computing skills and constant reference to the 'Guide to the Internet' I had saved from the Sunday newspaper, it had taken me less than half an hour to find a list of pubs and small hotels in the Flyncombe area. It was easy enough to find up-to-date information, but rather harder to find out about pub and hotel opening times in the 1950s.

Churches weren't any easier. I thought it quite likely that service times would be more or less set in stone and that if I found out the times of services now, then they would probably have been the same then. Of course, there may have been churches that had closed since then. I knew that the Quaker house I used to go to as a child no longer existed as a building, but when I last heard about it, people were meeting in each other's homes. That wasn't in Flyncombe, though, but ten miles further inland.

In the end, I sent an email to Flyncombe library, asking them if they had information about the area in the 1950s, including pubs and churches, or if not, could they put me in touch with a local historian. As soon as I had told the computer to 'send', I wondered how wise this was. Jim and

I were, in effect, investigating a suspicious death. I panicked.

All the counted breathing in the world couldn't control this one. My head was buzzing; my hands and feet were tingling. I was gasping and sweating and the room was swimming about me. I leant forward and put my head between my legs. It was a most undignified position, but effective to a certain extent. I grabbed an A4 envelope from the desk and breathed into it a few times. The room slowed down. I was able to stop hyperventilating and control my breathing again.

I sat up slowly and told myself not to be silly, that I was perfectly safe; this became a sort of mantra that I repeated over and over again. I prayed that God would protect me and Jim. I felt my body settle and respond. My heart resumed a regular rhythm. I slowly stretched my arms and then used the desk to pull myself up to a standing position. I was fine again.

I walked through to the kitchen to make myself a coffee while I mulled things over. Was I right? Were we putting ourselves in danger? Or was this one more example of me 'catastrophising', as Mike would say? I picked up the phone to ring Mike's receptionist and ask for an earlier appointment – maybe I wasn't quite ready to only see him once a fortnight.

I decided that I had done enough on trying to find out about Harry Standish. I had no idea when Jim would make contact and was beginning to doubt whether he would ring at all. So I was both pleased and nervous when Jim rang that evening. He was full of what he had discovered. He had been to the library and found some articles on microfiche which he had printed off. 'Jenny, you'll never believe what a lot of interest there was. The police seemed to be trying to quieten it all down, with lots of remarks about searching for the suicide note and asking the journalists to give the family space for their grief, but the reporters definitely seemed suspicious.'

I interrupted him, for the moment caught up in his enthusiasm, so forgetting to talk to him about my worries. 'Do you know who any of the journalists were?'

'Yes!' he announced with what sounded like triumph. 'I tracked one down, too. It wasn't difficult, as he still writes letters to the *Flyncombe News* and I had seen his name the other day so I recognised it. I looked him up in the phone book and there he was. He's Gerald Longwater and he still lives in Flyncombe. He is very interested that we are looking at Standish's suicide. He never believed it was suicide at the time.'

My heart sank – yet another person who knew we were looking closely at this. 'Jim,' I started, 'I'm getting worried.'

There was a pause on the line. 'What do you mean?'

'Well, if Standish's suicide was suspicious, and now we are investigating it, do you think that puts us in danger?'

'I wondered if you'd think that, Jenny. It occurred to me the other day. When I spoke to Gerald, I asked him not to tell anyone about our conversation, and I rang Freddie to say the same. It was a bit late with Freddie, though; he'd begun his own line of enquiries and had been asking all sorts of people about what they remembered.'

'Did he say why he was asking?'

'No, only that he'd met someone in the pub and they'd started chatting about it. I don't think he mentioned my name, and he doesn't even know yours, so you're safe, Jenny.'

Somehow I kept it all together. I told him I had emailed the library but hadn't said why I was researching local pubs and churches, just in case they might become suspicious.

'That's fine – no one will know why you are doing this. But if you're really concerned, why don't you have a bit of a cover story ready, in case anyone asks?'

We spent a few minutes throwing around ideas. In the end it was decided that I was writing a series of romantic short stories set in the 1950s and wanted to use some authentic settings.

'I hope they don't want to read any of these non-existent works of fiction!' I said, trying to think of the last time I had written a short story. Probably back in my school days.

'I shouldn't think so – you could always pick a magazine and say you're submitting the series to them.'

'Do women's magazines still publish short stories?'

Jim laughed. 'How do I know? I'll leave the research for your cover story to you! If you want to look really authentic, you might need a manuscript to scribble on when you go to your locations – so get writing!' He was still laughing.

'Very funny. Anyway, I wouldn't have time. I'm too busy playing detective. Well, helping *you* play detective.'

'Oh, I think you are very much part of this, Jenny. You seem to come up with all the things I hadn't noticed, like the churches.'

'I might be leading us up the garden path, though.'

'The whole thing might be a jaunt up a jolly garden path. We must keep sight of the fact that Standish's suicide might merely be that.'

I remembered the silhouetted man at the top of the cliff – the man standing tall, crossing himself, looking powerful.

'I'm going to take some convincing,' I said.

9

It wasn't long before Jim called back. In fact, it was less than two hours. He didn't even wait for me to say 'hello' when I picked up the phone, but immediately launched into a stream of ideas and information.

'I had a phone call from Henry's son. He's found his file of information on his father. He had loads of scraps of newspaper reports and feedback from the investigation that was used in the coroner's court. Just listen to this.'

'Hold on a minute, let me sit down.' I pulled the phone over to the side of a chair, grabbed my pen and notepad from the phone table and made myself comfortable. 'Right, I'm ready. Tell me all about it.'

'Well, you know Henry was in the police?'

'Yes.'

'He took early retirement and was becoming licensed to work as a private detective. You'll never guess what his first case was.'

'No idea. Divorce case? Anyway, why did he have a case if he wasn't licensed?'

'Wait, I'll explain. Henry had been working on the case of Dan Wallis while he was in the police. Dan Wallis killed himself, according to the coroner. '

'That's a coincidence.'

'Precisely. But the thing is, Dan was not depressed. He was looking forward to a holiday he was booked to go on the next day. He was trying to pack but received a phone call. He dropped everything, and the next thing he was dead.'

'So why was this not treated as suspicious?'

'He was alone and he jumped off a motorway bridge.'

'Jumped?'

'Well, two separate witnesses say he "dived" off the bridge.'

I felt a shudder down my spine. My breathing was fast again. 'Hang on a minute,' I managed to say. 'Give me a moment or two. I'll call you back.'

I hung up the phone and slowed my breathing. I went and found a drink of water. My head was chock-a-block with images – the usual one now overlaid with a second man diving off a bridge. Too similar to be a coincidence.

I looked up Jim's number and rang him back. 'Hi Jim, sorry about that. How come Henry was still working on this case after the coroner's verdict?'

'Dianne, Dan's wife, hired him. Officially he wasn't doing anything, of course, but he had made loads of handwritten notes, which were presumably from his work on the case while he was in the police.'

'Is that allowed?'

'I shouldn't think so. Freddie was sure that was what he was writing, because he was always at his desk scribbling away, and he had overheard his mother telling him he should leave "that case" alone now that the verdict had been given. Freddie especially remembers because he'd asked his dad to take him to a cricket match and his dad had said he would try, but he might be too busy. The date of the match was a few days after Henry died.'

'Did Freddie ever find any notes?'

'No, he thinks that's what the police were looking for.'

'What do you think happened, Jim?'

'I think Dan Wallis had discovered something that meant he had to be silenced, and Henry was on the point of finding out what that was.'

'But what? And who silenced them both?'

'That's the question we need to answer, Jenny.'

I didn't know what to say. I was so unsure of all this. I had felt a bit better while I had someone to talk to about it all, but this was too sinister. Too other-worldly. I wondered if Jim was as dependable as he seemed.

'This is getting very strange, Jim. I'm not sure we should be delving any deeper.'

'Jenny, we're really getting somewhere. We can't stop now.'

'Don't say that, Jim. We can stop, if we decide to.'

'I don't want us to,' said Jim slowly.

I wasn't sure if he was still talking about the case. Whatever it was, I certainly didn't feel on safe ground.

'I've a lot to think about. I'll ring you later,' was all I managed to say before I put the phone down.

I didn't ring him. He rang me later that evening.

'I'm sorry to ring you, Jenny, but I didn't want to leave you feeling pressurised into continuing with our detective work. '

'No, that's all right. I really like to take things slowly. You know, we don't know what we're getting into.'

As soon as I said it, I realised that I could have been talking about 'us'. It was fine; he realised I was talking about the case.

'We have found rather more than we expected, haven't we?'

'Yes, it's only two hours since you reminded me this could be a straightforward suicide. Do you think so now?'

There was hardly a pause before Jim replied. 'No, I do not. And I think we might have two suspicious deaths on our hands.'

'They're nothing to do with us. Maybe we should hand it all over to the police?' I suggested. I imagined what a relief this would be, but how frustrating not to know if anyone was investigating it.

There was silence for a few minutes. I tried to imagine what Jim might be thinking.

'I don't think I can do that, Jenny. But if you want out, then that's fine.'

'I don't know what I want.'

'Look, let's meet somewhere and talk face to face. I'm going to be in London for a few days next week staying with my brother-in-law, so perhaps you know of somewhere – a café, maybe?'

I knew I couldn't walk into a café to meet him. I hadn't been into one for years, apart from Jim's. In fact, managing to make the journey to the Tube to reach Mike's office had been the climax of my excursions on my own until the emergency with my aunt.

I took a deep breath. 'There's something I should tell you, Jim.' I paused and swallowed. 'I'm a recovering agoraphobic. I'm not good with outings unless I'm with my psychologist. The thing at the beach was a one-off. I can't cope with a café.'

'Oh, that's what it is. Hence the panic.'

'Partly, yes. But other things freaked me out that day.'

'That comes back to how childhood experiences affect us, does it?'

'Yes.' My voice sounded small. I was sure Jim would want to get away, yet he was still here, talking.

'In that case, is there anywhere else we can meet?'

I was so grateful that he didn't write me off that I forgot to be cautious. 'Why don't you come here? I'm not far from the Tube station.'

'That would be good, thank you very much. Would next Tuesday be all right, in the afternoon?'

I'd recovered enough to try to sort things out. 'Yes, of course. Three-ish? And will you have your wife with you?'

'My wife? No, I don't have a wife.'

'Oh, sorry, I simply presumed. You have a son?'

'Long story, I'll tell you over a cup of tea.'

10

I woke on the following Tuesday feeling queasy. Not because of the usual nightmare, but another one. In it I was standing on the shoreline with the sand and sea getting into my sandals, talking to Mike on the Dictaphone, while Jim was walking, or perhaps surfing, on the water, trying to reach me. His speckled hair was sparkly with drops of water. The waves were high and rolling, crashing onto the beach. Every time he rode on a wave to come nearer, he was pulled back by the undercurrent. I couldn't reach him. His arms were stretched out to balance him. I was standing by, helpless, telling Mike what was happening again and again.

The dream stayed with me while I was getting up – I couldn't eat any breakfast. By then I was beginning to panic and I nearly phoned Mike. But I thought better of it. I was trying so hard to deal with situations on my own.

I knew why I was so unnerved: I had made an utter fool of myself in inviting Jim to the house. If I didn't count Mike, when he first helped me with my agoraphobia, then it was the first time I had entertained a male visitor since my mother had died.

And how ridiculous to invite someone I had known for such a short time! What was I getting into? I tried to allay my fears by getting ready. By mid-morning I had given up cleaning everything in sight and was trying to decide whether to phone him to cancel. I dithered for too long, my failure to make a decision becoming the decision itself.

By quarter to two, I was sitting on the edge of one of my dining chairs wondering whether I should simply be out when he arrived. My own principles wouldn't allow it even if the agoraphobia would. Instead, I set myself the task of writing up the facts as we knew them so far, ready for the meeting. Perhaps if we kept everything really businesslike, I would be able to manage. I hoped it would calm my nerves.

Before long, I was engrossed. We had gathered more information than I thought. From pages of scribbled notes, I put together a list.

Henry Standish – suicide or sinister death?

1. Henry's family report he had no reason to commit suicide: no marriage problems, no mood problems, no financial difficulties. He was a devout Catholic who saw suicide as an unforgivable sin.

2. Henry's two closest friends agree it was a complete surprise and totally out of character. One friend, who had known him since their teenage years, said, 'He must have been ill or hallucinating.'

3. Henry Standish had told his wife he would be back later and said he would cook them all a roast meal then instead of at lunchtime, which was when they usually ate a main meal on a Sunday. He told his son he would look at his homework.

4. He said he was meeting someone that morning in Flyncombe. This person has never been traced and we don't know if the meeting took place. It was more usual for him to be home with his family or at church on a Sunday.

5. The police were very interested in his death and searched the café thoroughly, especially the roof. The *Devon News* reported that 'up to thirty' police officers carried out an inch-by-inch search of the surrounding areas. We do not know what they were looking for.

6. Henry had retired from the police and was in the process of being registered as a private detective. (Therefore, the interest the police had in his death may only have been because he was an ex-colleague.)

7. Although his registration had not come through, Henry had been hired by Dianne Wallis, the widow of Dan Wallis, who had also committed suicide under strange circumstances. She was convinced her husband had been murdered, even though he 'dived' off a motorway flyover and there were witnesses to say that he was alone.

8. The coroner returned a verdict of suicide for both Dan Wallis and Henry Standish.

9. Henry Standish had one son, Freddie, who says his father loved life and was always 'the life and soul of a party'. He had no reason to suspect that his father would commit suicide and still cannot accept it.

10. According to Freddie, his mother (Gloria Standish) never accepted the verdict.

11. Freddie says his father had accepted the Wallis case before being registered because it was a case he had previously worked on for the police but disagreed with the coroner's verdict of suicide.

12. Freddie has never found any notes from the Wallis case and thinks the police probably took them away.

This was all the old stuff Jim and I had already talked about as we had collected the information from people's recollections and newspaper cuttings over the last few weeks. But writing it down together made me think about the two suicides. I wondered if it had been the same coroner in each case.

I expected that Jim would have most of the detailed information.

I took out another piece of paper and wrote 'Theories' across the top and 'Questions' halfway down the page. Apart from the question about the coroner, and the theory that Henry Standish had found out something that someone was desperate for no one to know, that was it. We hadn't got very far.

I started to think the other way round. Maybe it was a suicide and the only reason the police had been hunting through his belongings was to make sense of it? Maybe he committed suicide because of something that was happening in the police force – perhaps that was why he had taken early retirement.

I got up and stretched – enough was enough. My back ached. I had been stooped over for too long. I did the shoulder exercises my mother made me do as a child to stop me from developing a hunched back like my grandmother. Then I made myself a sandwich. I hadn't eaten all day.

Only as I ate my late lunch did I realise I seemed to have made a decision. Somehow or another, I was working on this mystery whether I wanted to or not. I was still not sure it would be safe to do so, but then, who was I to judge? I didn't even think it was safe to walk out of my house and up the street to meet Jim in a café!

I pushed everything into a folder and went to brush my hair.

11

The minute I opened the door to Jim that afternoon, I felt better. Although we'd been talking over the phone and emailing each other, I had almost forgotten what he looked like, so it was rather like seeing him for the first time.

My first impression was that he had something comfortable about him – like an old pair of slippers. He's not what I would necessarily describe as a good-looking man, but there's nothing wrong with him, either. He's about five feet ten inches tall. He has a warm smile that spreads slowly across his slightly chubby face, giving him dimples in both cheeks. His slightly wavy hair is not very grey, but quite dark, dashed with silver. Good thick hair, a bit wiry. That day he was wearing a brown jacket with a smart pair of jeans. On his shoulder was a rather battered khaki canvas messenger bag.

'Hi there, Jenny. Good to see you. You're looking great!'

I felt quite awkward. I could feel heat rising up into my face – it was rare for me to get anything approaching a compliment. Then I remembered that the previous time I had seen him I'd been distraught and gasping for breath. Anyone would look great after the snivelling wretch I had been then. This time I had taken a bit of care over my appearance, choosing my favourite teal jumper and a brown straightish skirt with a coordinating silk scarf my aunt had bought me for Christmas.

I tried to keep my voice steady. 'Thank you, Jim. It's good to see you, too. Come on in. I'll put the kettle on for some coffee or tea, shall I?'

'Yes, thanks. Mine's tea with one sugar, if that's okay.'

He followed me up the hall and into the kitchen, which felt a bit unnerving. After all, I didn't really know him very well. I felt my breathing speed up.

'Anything I can do?' said Jim. 'Or would you rather I keep out of your way?'

'You go and sit in there,' I said, pointing to the sitting room. I didn't mean it to sound curt, but I think it did a little.

By the time I took the tea in, Jim was sat in the middle of the sofa, busily spreading out all his papers on the coffee table. I placed the tray on the sideboard behind him and sat opposite, on one of the easy chairs. I realised I had practically an all-round view of Jim, with the reflection of the back of his head in the sideboard mirror. I couldn't think of anything to say to him, so quietly sat and waited, trying not to watch his reflection.

'We need to make some sort of list, I think, of what we've found out and what we can do next,' he said.

'I've started one,' I told him, reaching for my handwritten notes.

He took them from me, put on a pair of half-glasses and began to read it. He kept raising his thick dark eyebrows and giving me a little smile as he went through. 'Not much I can add to that, really. Although I do have the articles on

Wallis' death with me, if you're interested. Oh, and I might even have the name of the coroner.'

Of course I was interested!

We looked at the articles first. They were quite brief. First there was a report of the actual event. I read through this several times, trying to see if there was anything religious about the suicide. I hadn't been able to get out of my mind the image of Henry Standish crossing himself. There was nothing. The only thing that was unusual about Wallis was the fact that he seemed to dive off the flyover, not jump.

'Do you know anything about people committing suicide?' I asked Jim.

'No, not really.'

'Well, both our people did something strange: Henry Standish crossed himself and held his arms out to the side, and Wallis was described as diving off the flyover. Do people do that? I always imagined they leaped into the air.'

'Henry crossed himself?'

I felt foolish that I hadn't told him already. 'Yes, I'm sure he did.'

Jim asked me to describe what I had seen as a six-year-old. I had to take time, controlling my breathing as I talked. Slowly, I went over it, trying to remember as clearly as I could across the years. As I did so, I began to worry that I might have distorted it as I grew up.

I reached the point where he jumped. I was struggling to talk by then. My hands were hot and sticky. I pulled out my hanky to surreptitiously wipe them.

Jim leaned forward, watching and waiting. 'Sorry, Jenny. I didn't realise how hard this would be. Look, write stuff down when you feel ready, if you'd rather. Or tell me another time.'

I realised my hanky was a screwed-up ball in my hand.

''Scuse me,' I mumbled as I stumbled out of the room, desperately trying to keep myself steady.

I went upstairs to the bathroom. I sat on the edge of the bath, concentrating on my feelings, trying to calm my body and my mind. When my breathing was calmer, I washed my face and brushed my hair. So much for the careful application of make-up earlier in the day. I straightened my skirt and went back to the sitting room. I started to speak as I went through the door, desperate to let him know what happened, but not trusting myself to keep calm.

'What I particularly remember is that he crossed himself,' I showed him on myself, 'and then he spread his arms out to the side and sort of pushed himself upwards.'

'As if he were trying to fly?'

Relief flooded me. I gulped and bit my lip. I could feel my eyes moisten. I had felt so foolish thinking that for all these years. Yet here was someone else interpreting those actions in the same way that I did. I nodded.

'Yes, yes. Exactly as if he were trying to fly. I was only six and it was what I thought he was doing when I saw it happen.' I didn't think I had better say that the thought was so powerful that I was sure I would be able to fly and had broken my leg trying to copy him.

'I wonder what was going through his mind.'

'I don't know. How would anyone know?'

'There must be studies about people who have tried to kill themselves but failed. You said you'd been seeing a psychologist, didn't you?'

I nodded – I had rather hoped Jim had forgotten that. 'Yes. I don't see him as often as I did. I'm much better these days, but I will be seeing him next week.'

'Good. He might be able to help us. Do you think he'd be able to tell us if Standish's behaviour was strange? Or Wallis', for that matter? We could do with understanding this better.'

I thought about Mike's room with its untidy muddle of papers and journals. His shelves were bowed with their loads of books, including some with titles associated with depression. 'I should think he'll know,' I said. 'I'll ask him.'

I found I was enjoying having Jim in my front room. I made more tea and bravely produced my home-made scones with jam and cream. Talk turned away from the mystery while we ate. I usually hated eating in front of anyone else, but maybe that was because I was not used to it. With Jim it felt different.

Jim talked about the weather while I poured tea. He described the surfers who were now frequent visitors to his café and the fact that thanks to them the café was flourishing. I wanted to ask him about his son. I was formulating questions in my mind but somehow lacked the courage to ask them. But it was as if he read my mind.

'It's a shame I have no one to pass it on to,' said Jim, 'now that it's picked up.'

'Isn't your son interested?'

'I don't think he'd manage it. And he's not officially my son.'

'Is he your stepson?'

'No, he's my sister's youngest.' He paused, perhaps wondering if he should explain himself.

'Oh, I see,' I said, although I wasn't sure that I did.

Jim half-shrugged and began to speak again. 'My sister died in childbirth, leaving my brother-in-law with two daughters and Stephen, who was a sickly baby but survived. My brother-in-law couldn't cope.'

'So, did you bring Stephen up?'

'He went into care at first. He was born with Down's syndrome and he wasn't really progressing at all. I asked for contact visits to begin with, then I became more and more involved. He was a lovely little fellow, always smiling. He was placed with a single lady and, probably because there weren't any other men in his life, he called me Dad.'

I wasn't surprised; there was something quite paternal about Jim.

'Hence you refer to him as your son. Where does he live now?'

'He's lived with me from the age of six. The foster carer took on three sisters and Stephen became unhappy. They began to look for another foster home and I couldn't stand the thought of him moving to someone he didn't know, so I asked to become his carer.'

He was telling me all this about himself with a tone of complete humility. I realised I was staring at him, probably open-mouthed. I could not imagine being so generous myself. I managed to speak. 'How did you cope?'

'With difficulty! Stephen has always needed a lot of help, so that can be hard work. Luckily he was taken to school at eight-thirty and wasn't back until four-thirty, so these became the café hours. I merely had to fit my life around his. His father had him some Saturdays, and my parents helped a bit. So we got by with a great deal of prayer.'

'I'm really impressed,' I said.

Jim looked at me, his blue eyes soft. 'I hope you meet him one day,' he said. 'If you do, you'll see why I wanted to look after him.'

I smiled at him. I was relaxed in his presence, but that didn't mean I could become involved in his life. I thought it best not to comment.

We descended into chit-chat while we continued eating scones. I carried the tray back to the kitchen. Meanwhile, Jim spread out an A3 sheet of paper which he started to cover with odd words and notes. Planning our next move had begun.

12

Jim stayed so long that day that I ended up offering him some tinned tomato soup and rolls. I wished I'd known it would be such a lengthy meeting, because my home-made soup is quite good and I hadn't had reason to make it since my mother died. I would have liked the opportunity. But he seemed really grateful to be offered even this meagre meal.

I laid the table for two in the dining room. The room was cold and seemed slightly damp from disuse. Jim saw me coming down the stairs carrying the fan heater. 'Don't warm the room up for me; I don't feel the cold.'

'No, it's all right. I'll leave it on for a bit while the soup's warming.'

I took my time heating the soup and microwaving the rolls to thaw them. I was pleased I had some real butter and not only marge. It was my treat the previous time I phoned through an order to my local store. They had been delivering for years now; I was still not ready to shop.

I thawed plenty of rolls and found a few things to go on bread in case he was hungry. I don't know what he was expecting, but I put my fruit bowl on the table too, plus some cheese and biscuits. All the time I was trying to think what men ate in the evening. A main meal probably, but I didn't have anything in to manage that.

I called Jim through to the dining room, remembering to switch off the fan heater.

'This looks good,' he said, looking at the table. I thought he was probably being polite.

'If you sit here,' I said indicating the far side of the table, 'then I can easily fetch anything I've forgotten.'

Jim took a seat. I sat on my chair, but didn't start eating. I was in a quandary: should my guest eat first, or was he waiting for me?

'Are we waiting to say grace?' asked Jim. I shook my head. 'No? It's only that I usually say it with Stephen.'

'Please do if you want to.'

Jim smiled. 'Don't worry,' he said. 'I'm sure God knows by now that I'm grateful to him – and to you too on this occasion!' He picked up his spoon and began to eat his soup.

I toyed with mine a bit, suddenly self-conscious. It hadn't occurred to me that he might say grace. I wondered if he really did say it with Stephen, or whether it was me describing the sign of the cross that had made him think he should. But by now Jim had buttered a roll and seemed to be relishing every spoonful of his soup. He was too busy eating to ask him, and I wasn't sure I should. I made myself relax, and began to eat.

By the time we had reached the cheese and biscuits, I had learned quite a lot about Jim. Well, mainly about Stephen, as Jim described some of his difficulties in the past and the part-time job he now had in a supermarket as a cleaner. Jim seemed really proud of him, and I became caught up in his enthusiasm. He certainly seemed to love that boy.

There seemed little to do except clear up after we had eaten. Jim rolled up his scribbling, which now included the plan, divided into tasks allocated to each of us. I still felt uneasy about what we were doing. 'What happens if we stir something up that we can't cope with?' I asked.

Jim ignored my clumsy sentence. 'I don't think we will. We're talking about something that happened fifty years ago, and most of the people concerned will either be very old or dead. Even the police are not interested. It's an old case, which in their opinion is a closed case.'

'I'm really unsure about it all.'

'Look, you can bow out at any time. I will carry on. We have uncovered a mystery and I for one want to solve it. But I don't want you to be involved against your will.'

Looking at his smile, I felt more confident. 'I'm in it for now, but if I become really uneasy I will talk to you before bailing out.'

'Thank you, Jenny. Although it may be me who bails out – you never know. And of course, there may be no mystery at all, but we will never feel comfortable about it unless we have tried to find out the truth.'

'I suppose you're right. But you had better get back to your brother-in-law.'

'Yes, and Stephen.' Jim looked at his watch. 'Oops! I am rather late. Would you mind if I used your phone?'

While he phoned I took our dirty plates into the kitchen. I was already beginning to wonder if this was the end of a great adventure. I couldn't hear what he was saying to his brother-in-law, but in my mind I was interpreting it as an excuse, something like, 'The old bat wouldn't let me get away.' I stopped this line of thought, though. Hadn't Dr Lewis, Mike, told me that this was a very non-productive way of thinking? I didn't know what Jim was saying and I had no thought-reading powers.

I made myself leave the kitchen and go to talk to Jim. There was one more awkward moment to negotiate as I saw him out.

'Thank you so much,' he said. 'It's been lovely to get to know you a bit as well as move forward on unravelling the mystery.'

'Yes, Jim, it's been good to get together.' I couldn't take the words back, and I didn't know if he would read anything into what I'd said. I added, 'You know, to work on finding out what really happened.'

'I hope I haven't outstayed my welcome.'

'No, that's fine. I haven't anything special planned this evening.'

'Well, goodbye, Jenny. I'll ring you as soon as I discover anything interesting.'

'Yes, that would be good.' I stopped myself from saying, *I'll look forward to that*. The whole afternoon had felt strangely intimate, yet very much at arm's length. So peculiar. I really hoped I would meet up with Jim again.

13

I woke up early the next day with a strange feeling of warmth and contentment. It took me a while to remember that I had spent so long with Jim in my own house. I lay in bed thinking about how good it had felt to have someone else to share a meal and talk with.

Then doubts crept in. What had I done? I had been alone with a strange man for an afternoon and half the evening. I didn't even know him. I began to have all the old thoughts I used to have about going mad.

I got myself up, trying to rationalise my thinking. Mike had taught me to question my thoughts. I wasn't sure this would help, because however you looked at it I had placed myself in danger. Or had I? I had certainly taken a risk.

By the time I had eaten some breakfast – my usual standby, porridge cooked in the microwave – I had begun to think a little more positively. Jim was a new friend who had turned out to be someone rather special. He had taken on his dead sister's handicapped child and brought him up. He was still looking after him now he was an adult. I made a quick note to myself that I didn't actually know how old Stephen was. It may be that he had been a late baby and might not even be in his twenties yet. I didn't know. But Jim was a kind fellow. Obviously likeable, he was intelligent and had a good sense of humour.

I stopped this line of thinking immediately, realising that I was sounding like one of those adverts you read in a lonely hearts column. Was Jim a lonely heart?

With the sudden shock of the rising of a dormant thought, I realised that I was very much a lonely heart. I'd been too many years nursing my parents, God bless them. Then too many years unable to get out of the house. My loneliness was consuming me, leeching life from me.

I walked into my rarely used sitting room feeling very much alone. There on my coffee table lay a list in Jim's scrawly handwriting, detailing the tasks that had been left for me. I picked it up and crumpled it in my hand. If attempting to unravel a mystery was going to give me so much pain, then it was best left. I couldn't cope with more emotions in my life. I threw the list into the wastepaper bin.

My mood didn't lift all morning. Next door's cat came mewing at the door. I ignored him. Some mornings I would place a saucer of milk just outside the door. Today, the very act of pulling back the bolt felt beyond me. I needed to feel safe in my own home, with nothing disturbing me.

The phone rang. My phone was in the hall and difficult to ignore. But this time I walked into the kitchen and put the kettle on. It was too early for elevenses, but it helped to drown the noise. The ringing stopped and I walked into the sitting room, putting the radio on in case the phone rang again. I was feeling exhausted. I noticed crumbs on the floor but left them.

During the rest of the morning, I ignored the phone three more times. I tried reading, but couldn't concentrate. I eventually swept up the crumbs, using only the dustpan and brush. I tried writing my thoughts and challenging them. It was hopeless; I couldn't focus my mind. I attempted to stop thinking about Jim, but whatever I did reminded me of him. The mirror on the sitting room wall. The dining room chairs. To my horror I realised my silk scarf was draped across the chair I had used. Did I take off my scarf while I was talking to Jim? I was terrified I might have done. How would he have interpreted that action?

In the end, I gave in and let myself think about Jim. He was a lovely man and as far as I knew he had no expectations of me. He was single, which was strange, but probably because he had looked after a handicapped child, and I was single because I had nursed both parents until they died.

This was the moment when I realised we were both in the same boat. I took the crumpled list out of the bin and straightened it out to read it.

Jim had obviously taken some thought with its heading: 'Proposed list for Jenny, should she want to help.'

I smiled. He had known my reluctance before we had spoken about it. Was he on the same wavelength as me, or was I so transparent? I didn't know if that mattered, really; he was obviously being considerate in giving me a let-out.

There wasn't too much on the list to surprise me. I had already agreed to ring one or two people, and the only new one was Gloria, Henry's wife. Jim had said that Freddie thought she would rather speak to a woman and would warn her that I might contact her. I was unsure about this but thought I could manage a phone call.

My research tasks were varied, mostly extending searches I had already done. I didn't mind; it reminded me of projects at school, although they were all pre-internet. Back then I would love to spend time in the reference section of the library, hunting for particular quotes, or even taking out books to pore over at home. My essays were always too long, stuffed full of non-essential facts that were important to me so had to be recorded somewhere. I was never particularly good at sticking to task.

The phone rang again and this time I answered it, still thinking about school days. It was Jim, of course.

'Oh, you're there, thank goodness,' he said. 'I've been trying to get hold of you and when no one answered the phone, I wondered what had happened.'

Guilt nearly overwhelmed me. It had simply not occurred to me that he might be worried if I didn't answer. I couldn't remember the last time anyone was worried about me. 'I'm sorry. I wasn't answering the phone. I needed time to think.'

I expected Jim to tell me off, or maybe sound cross. But instead he said, 'I'm so relieved you're all right. You need an answerphone message telling people you are resting and will ring back later.'

'I'm sorry.'

'No, don't apologise. I shouldn't have presumed to ring you. It's completely up to you if you don't want to answer the phone. I'm sorry I disturbed you. I'd better ring off.'

'No, don't. I'm all right now; I'm happy to talk. Have you found something out already?'

'Well, no. I only wanted to thank you for putting up with me for so long yesterday. And to check that you weren't left too exhausted by it all. It occurred to me that you might not get many visitors if you don't ever go out to see people, so I'm feeling guilty.'

'I enjoyed you being here.' My mind was trying to stop me saying anything that could be taken the wrong way, so I added, 'It made a change to be entertaining again.' That sounded worse: he'd come to work on the mystery, not to be entertained.

'Well, I enjoyed being there. You looked after me well.' There was a silence, which I was unsure how to fill. He spoke again, slowly. 'Look, Jenny, I was wondering if you ever get out and if so whether I could meet you and we could maybe spend time somewhere together.'

I couldn't think what he meant for a minute or two. Then fear changed my tone of voice as I replied, 'You know I find it difficult to get anywhere. I wouldn't be comfortable meeting you somewhere.'

'I'm sorry, Jenny. I merely thought we got on well and I enjoyed talking to you. I'll ring you when I have something to report back on. Bye for now.'

I didn't even have time to say goodbye before there was a click as he put down his receiver. I sat on the stairs still holding the phone. Why on earth had I upset this lovely man? He was only trying to be kind. I felt useless.

14

It was the morning of my extra appointment with Mike and I ate my breakfast with the normal feeling of dread. Speaking to Mike was helpful, sometimes life-changing, but getting there was a real challenge, and I was never sure whether I would cope. Twice in the past I hadn't even reached the Tube station. When I had rushed back home, it had taken a while to ring the office to say I hadn't made it. Mike always rang back and we more or less had a session over the phone. But I knew that it would have been better face to face and that I had backslidden once again.

With my appointment at eleven o'clock, I pushed myself out of the house at ten. My garden path looked a mess. Weeds were straggling out between the slabs. I decided that later today I would try to do something about it. The rest of the small front garden was now lawn with a few shrubs. My gardener was due next week, but the lawn already looked long and neglected. I realised that Jim had stood at my door yesterday and probably wondered what state the house would be in, considering the mess in the garden.

I went through the gate and paused for breath. I noticed my breathing had become shallow and quick, so I slowed it down. The gentleman from two doors down was watching me, so I covered up my pause with a glance through my handbag as if checking that I hadn't forgotten anything. I nearly went back in, but instead managed to wave at my neighbour and walk on.

While I was stood by the gate, a young woman had passed me with a small child in a pushchair. The little girl now leant round her mother and waved at me. I didn't know her but I managed to smile a little. She then sat upright, where she couldn't see me, then peeped round again. Somehow, the child's spontaneous game of peek-a-boo helped me to keep pace a few yards behind her mother. That was how I reached Kennington Station.

It's always a bit easier indoors – even in a busy place like a Tube station. I didn't need a distraction to stay there. I bought my ticket and joined the crowds going down to the Northern line. Even on the Tube itself it was strangely easier than outdoors, although I suffered the usual inconvenience of a busy train. I did find a seat, although I had to put up with a large lady pushing her suitcase against my legs as the train filled up. Even if I'd had the courage to ask her to move, it wouldn't have helped: there was no space behind her. I had a book with me, and I looked at an open page, manoeuvring my legs out of the way as far as I could. I never read on the Tube; I would simply open the book to avoid meeting anyone's eyes.

Emerging out of the Tube, with several streets to walk to Mike's department, I was pleased to see it was raining. I have a transparent umbrella with a high centre, which creates my own space within its shape. It makes me feel separated from the outside world just enough to make the walk bearable. I sometimes pray for rain so that I won't look silly if I use my umbrella. The first time I managed to make my own way to Mike's office, I had used the refuge of its thin layer of plastic, despite the glorious sunshine, but it had been difficult to ignore the stares of other pedestrians.

Mike had no one in his office when I arrived, so he called me in. I sat on the newest of his shabby armchairs, the one closest to the door. He seemed to have tidied up a bit, and his piles of papers and files were greatly reduced. His plant on the filing cabinet still looked in need of water and dolefully sat surrounded by coffee mugs. Mike picked up a file from his desk and walked round the coffee table to the other armchair.

'How are you today, Jenny, and is there a reason for this earlier appointment?' Mike stroked his red beard as he spoke. Even that looked as if it had been trimmed.

'I'm not sure how I am. I managed to get here today by playing peek-a-boo with a toddler while I walked to the Tube, then by staying under my brolly from the Tube to here.'

I'm sure Mike knew I was buying time. 'How are you generally? You asked for this extra appointment.'

I felt a bit silly. Could I really start talking to Mike about the fact that I was possibly – no, probably – becoming attracted to a man? And could I explain to him that I had invited Jim to my house and thus put myself in danger? Sitting here in this office with a man who saw all sorts of people with huge mental health issues, it all seemed rather petty.

He was waiting for an answer. 'I suppose I was thinking I had put myself at risk and that I might have upset a friend.'

'Go on.'

'You know the man I met in the café who remembered that incident?' Mike nodded. 'Well, we started emailing and we found more things that didn't add up. We spoke on the phone a few times and he had started to talk to people. So he came to my house to put together our findings and make a plan.'

Mike sat up, looking concerned. 'So he arrived on your doorstep uninvited? From Devon? How did he get your address?'

'No, no. Jim's not like that. He asked whether we could meet somewhere, because he would be in London for a few days. Of course I couldn't do that, so I suggested he came round...'

'Oh, I see, by invitation. So why are you worried about this? Did something terrible happen?'

'No, nothing. It's simply that, well, I don't know, really. I suppose I had a strange man in my house and I was on my own, so I put myself at risk.'

'I see. What would someone positive, an outsider, say to you?'

I recognised the cognitive therapy question and smiled. 'It depends who it was, I suppose. If it were someone really confident they would say, "Good for you," but if it were someone else who lived on their own, well, I'm not sure.'

'Do you think it's right to take some small risks in life?'

'That's the problem, Mike. It feels like a really big risk to step out of the door to get here. So I've lost all sense of proportion.'

'Ideally, you would meet someone new in a safe place, like a café. But as you don't think that's an option for you yet, then I guess you took a small risk in having him come to your house. Did you try to lessen the risk at all?'

I thought for a moment. How could I have done that? I didn't have any friends to be in the house. I could scarcely have used my psychologist as a back-up, although his phone numbers were stored in my phone – even his home number, which I had never used.

'I have your phone number in my house. His whole name was written in my diary. Nothing else.'

'Well, there was one thing you had already done.'

'What's that?'

'Remember what you told me had led up to this?'

I tried to remember what I had said. 'I suppose I got to know him a bit.'

'Yes, you must have formed a favourable opinion of him, or you would never have suggested he came to the house. If you're unsure about him being there, what could you put in place for next time?'

'I don't think there will be a next time.'

'Didn't you like him, then?'

'Oh yes – very much!' I felt myself blush. I looked at my hands, hoping Mike didn't notice. Mike shuffled his papers for a bit before saying, 'Well, what's the problem?'

I told him about the phone call when Jim suggested we meet somewhere, and what I had said. Mike was nodding as I spoke, and pulling at his beard. It occurred to me that he might be trying not to laugh.

'Well, let's unpick this. You are unhappy because you may have offended a friend who thought he would buy you a nice cup of tea and a cream cake, probably to return the compliment of you plying him with... scones, maybe?'

I remembered the first time Mike had come to see me. I didn't know what people did when a psychologist came, so I had offered him scones with jam, followed by cake. He struggled to write notes and eat and talk at the same time.

'Yes, scones with jam and cream!' We were both smiling now.

'Do you pass a café on the way to the Tube station?'

'No, but I think there's one a little further up the road, past the station.'

'Then you have some homework. When you go home, you are to walk to the café and then walk home. You will know then that you can manage it the other way.'

'How will that help? I've told him "no".'

'If you find it easy, then you ring him tonight. If it's a problem, then you practise for a week and then ring him and tell him you have conquered walking to the café.'

'I can't leave him upset for a week.'

'Then ring him tonight and tell him you're working on it.'

I got out my notebook and Mike and I began breaking the task into small steps, in the way we had when we worked on me tackling the journey to his office. It didn't take long; in fact, I did most of the work myself. It looked so easy on paper.

'What else did you find out this morning that might help you?' asked Mike.

'That I need to follow a mother with a child who likes playing peek-a-boo.'

Mike laughed. 'There may not be one of those every time you step out of your front door. But you're along the right lines.'

'All right, I need a distraction each time I try something new or a little bit scary. I need to remember those positive thoughts too; I'm not sure I used them today.'

'Probably because you had other things on your mind.'

'I suppose I did.' We both knew that I had another *persbn* on my mind today. I reckoned I could ring him and tell him I could work on getting to the café. I hoped it was clean and sold good cakes.

Or, for that matter, that I could get there. I really wanted to have even the smallest of outings with Jim.

15

Going home on the Tube was easier than on the way; it was less crushed. I didn't even pretend to look at my book. Instead I got out my notebook and wrote a few more sentences to help me walk to the cafe. I repeated them over and over in my head as if they were a mantra. 'I am perfectly safe. I will look at the shops on the way. I can do this.'

Unfortunately, it had stopped raining when I left the Tube station. I felt exposed but, determined, I turned towards the café. There was a new shop immediately next to the station – well, it was new to me; it may have been there for years. It had pretty banners and cream jugs in the window. I didn't stop to look; I was already struggling to keep going. My breathing was all wrong. I could see the café, further away than I remembered. There was a bench and table outside on the pavement. It looked more like a pub. Not suitable at all. I stopped.

This is stupid, I thought. *I'm struggling to reach a place that I would never have wanted to go to if it hadn't been for Jim.* I remembered Jim's hand touching mine in the beach café. 'I can do this,' came into my mind, and I clung to the thought as if it were Jim's hand.

When I reached the bench, I was exhausted. I sat on it, then realised it was wet so stood up again. I was wearing my mac, and I swivelled round to try to see the back of me. It looked like I now had a round soggy bottom imprint. Panic was rising; I steadied myself with one hand on the back of the bench. When I was ready, I forced myself to turn around and look into the building. It wasn't exactly Ye Olde Tea Shoppe, more like a greasy spoon. I turned round and, fighting to control my panic, I made my way back home.

My mind was full of negatives. I was angry with myself for even thinking about meeting Jim and with Mike for encouraging me. I became desperate to get home to safety. I was walking so fast I was nearly running. As I walked, my mind became focused on one thing – to get indoors. I turned into my gate and came to the door. I felt sick. I struggled to find the keys, then had to fiddle with the lock, my hands were shaking so much. There was no relief when I stepped through and slammed the door, quickly drawing across the bolts.

Even once through my front door, it took some time to calm myself down. I leant my back against it, using all the strategies I could to settle myself. I counted as slowly as I could. I tried telling myself I was safe, then remembered I should be using that when outside. I kept telling myself that I had managed it: I had found the café. I was unconvinced. I found myself reciting bits of the Lord's Prayer. My back slid down the door until I was crouching. I began to cry. With the tears, the tension began to leave my body.

When I was ready, I went upstairs and washed my face, then combed my hair. It reminded me of when I panicked with Jim in the house. That time I coped, and I enjoyed his visit. I told myself that I had calmed myself before, so could do it again.

Feeling better, I went downstairs and made myself some soup for lunch. I took it to my desk, then sat at my computer and began to email Jim. I would have to tell him we couldn't meet. It took me a long time to decide what to write. Working on it shaped my thoughts. I desperately wanted to see him. The sentences morphed into a less final tone. It took nearly half an hour before I had an email that was possibly sendable:

> *Dear Jim*
> *I'm sorry if I sounded rude when you suggested we meet for a coffee. It's fear, that's all. I struggle more than you can imagine when I have to go out. I'm working on it. My psychologist set me a task of practising getting to the nearest café. I just about did it today, but it is awful. I panicked but I did get back home.*

I read it through. It didn't seem very friendly and made me sound as if I was really losing the plot. Well, I *had* lost it. It would have to do.

I didn't know how to finish, so after trying out multiple options, including 'Jenny Drake', 'Your friend Jenny', 'Love Jenny' and 'Sincerely, Jenny', I simply put, 'Jenny'.

I pressed 'send' before I could change my mind. Then I went into the kitchen to throw away my cold soup and find something else to eat.

During the afternoon, I must have checked the computer about thirty times. Silly, really; he was probably working in the café, or maybe he was still at his brother-in-law's house. After all, he said he'd be there for 'a few days', and I didn't know when the days started.

It wasn't until after I had watched the six o'clock news that I found he had replied.

Dear Jenny
Don't worry, I'm not offended, although at first I did wonder whether I had made such a bad impression that you had given up on me.
I'm surprised you didn't like the café. I popped into the one right next to the Tube station on my way to you last time – it is a gift shop as well – I was a bit early to come straight to you so I went in and browsed. It's full of candles and pretty presents for ladies. It is charming, in its way. It's the one with jugs in the window.
Is that the same one? If you don't like it, perhaps we could find somewhere else. Do you manage to go further afield if you have someone with you? I could always 'call for you'!
But afternoon tea or a cup of coffee are not essential to our friendship. So let me know if you'd rather leave the refreshments out while we concentrate on being sleuths!
God bless,
Jim

Relief flooded through me, quickly followed by thoughts about how stupid I was. If I had walked slowly I might have recognised that we had a new café along that block of shops. Without even thinking that it might look too pushy, I emailed back.

> *Dear Jim*
> *I went straight past that shop but was so fixed on reaching the place I knew that I didn't notice it was a café as well. With your positive recommendation I would like to see it.*
> *I am used to getting to the Tube station so I'm sure I could get there next time you're in London.*
> *Thank you,*
> *Jenny*

I resolved to read through the crumpled list and start on my tasks as soon as possible.

16

I wasn't sure what time would be best to talk to Gloria. She lived alone, but she was into her nineties, according to Jim. It felt quite rude to be talking to someone about their husband's suicide so many years ago. Perhaps I should tell her what I saw when I was six and see what she said.

I sat on the chair by the phone, fiddling with the curly wire. I passed the phone from hand to hand. The longer I left it, the more unsure I became about ringing. In the end I went and made myself a coffee, then came back, sat down with a new sense of purpose and rang at about eleven. I judged that to be a time between morning coffee and lunch.

The phone was picked up immediately. 'Hello, who is it?' were the first words spoken in a refined accent by a lady who sounded like a headmistress.

I nearly put the phone down, but instead I began to explain myself. 'My name is Jenny Drake, and I believe your son, Freddie, told you I might ring. I was a small child when your husband died, and I was there on the beach.'

'Sorry, dear, you'll have to speak up. Who did you say you are?'

I repeated what I had said, but slightly louder. I didn't want to shout, in case it sounded aggressive.

'So you're the one who saw him crossing himself? Why didn't you come forward at the inquest?'

'I was six years old. I don't know that I even knew there was an inquest.'

'Well, why do you want to tell me about it now?'

I thought, *Good point. Maybe I'll take the hint and say goodbye.* But having got this far, I carried on.

'Jim, the man who spoke to Freddie, thought it might help you to know that I have a very clear recollection of that day and that now I am an adult, I think it highly unlikely that he wanted to commit suicide.'

'Well, that makes two of us. Three with your friend. Four with my son. We never thought Henry would do anything like that. He was a religious man and he loved life. He had a passion for solving mysteries, like you and your friend.'

This was a novel thought, that I had a passion for anything. I liked that.

'I suppose we do. Well, at least this mystery. But I really don't want us to intrude on you. If you want us to back off, then please say so, and we will.'

'In most ways I got over it years ago – but I never for one moment thought that coroner was correct. Henry loved us and would not have left us destitute. The life insurance was invalid because of the verdict.'

'That's so wrong.'

'I'm not losing any sleep over it now. We got by, my son and I. Somehow we made it. I'm very proud of him, you know. Have you met him?'

'Well, no. Jim has, though, and he seemed impressed.'

'Well, you must meet him too. Fine young man. Never grew up under the shadow of his dad's suicide because he knew it wasn't true.'

'It can't have been easy bringing him up on your own.'

'Extraordinarily hard, I can tell you. But he already had a scholarship to the grammar school. So that was a help. He had extra grants for further tuition, too. Good investment for the school; he was an A1 pupil. A credit to them.'

'And to you, I should think.'

'Quite right. But I want to hear what you think happened.'

'It's what I saw that I'd like to try to tell you.' I was beginning to doubt my ability to talk about it at all.

'Go on then.'

So I told her. I needed a few breaks to steady myself along the way. Once she said, 'Carry on when you're ready,' but otherwise she quietly listened.

I described the picnic, the little pool with shells round it, the man on the cliff and how he walked backwards and forwards before crossing himself and raising his arms. I even told her how I thought he was trying to fly. I had tried to tell the adults, but they thought I was playing because I usually was. I stopped when I talked about the Sea Rescue helicopter. She didn't need to know I had wanted to fly too.

There was a silence. I became worried that I may have upset Gloria so much that she had collapsed or something. Maybe I should have asked her to fetch a neighbour before I told her?

My heart was racing. I was about to ask her if she was all right, when she spoke. 'You were six,' she said. 'Jolly observant for six. And you still remember it.'

'Yes, I do. Vividly.'

'It had an effect on you, then.'

I didn't want to tell her about my agoraphobia, or my general fear of life. Not even that I had jumped off the breakwater and broken my leg. 'Yes, I suppose so,' was all I said.

She made a sort of *harrumph* noise, then told me, 'He was investigating circumstances around someone diving off a motorway bridge. It was a bit like you have described, except he didn't cross himself. Arms out and back, then he dived.'

'Do you know if he found anything out?'

'He said it involved a big company and he was not sure if he'd find out anything more.'

'I'm sorry to have brought all this up again for you.'

'It's always there, dear, underneath. Even when we think we are over it. But you have made me even more sure that it wasn't suicide.'

'In what way?'

'Henry would have chosen a less public way to die, if he had planned suicide. He would know the beach would be full of children and he would never, ever have traumatised a child. He loved children and a lot of his work in the police had been in protecting them. He refused to ever arrest a man in front of his children. He said it mucked them up for the rest of their lives.'

'He sounds a lovely man. I wish I'd known him.'

'He was, dear, he was.'

I didn't know what to say. To offer condolences at this late stage seemed inappropriate. I couldn't think how to end the conversation. I was sure I should have asked her some questions, but I couldn't remember what. Maybe Jim had written some instructions but I had left the crumpled list somewhere, probably by the kettle. The silence seemed to stretch down the phone line.

'You still there, dear? You've gone very quiet.'

'Yes, I am. Sorry, I was thinking. Is there anything you remember in the way of clues as to what might have happened?' Such a clumsy sentence, I felt embarrassed to have spoken it.

'Your friend asked my son to speak to me about that, and I said "no" but I forgot about the papers.'

'Which papers?'

'I have a box file of Henry's.'

'You do? Freddie thought the police took away all the papers.'

'They didn't come straight away to search the house. I popped Henry's box file round to my neighbour for safekeeping. I took round her usual hot dinner and put the box file in her little dining room with all her letters and bills. Henry had always said he didn't want anyone to see his research, not even his old colleagues, under any circumstances.'

'Did she, your neighbour, know what they were?'

'I don't think she ever discovered they were there. She mainly listened to the radio in her kitchen chair. She was over ninety and not very mobile. I used to help her up the stairs at bedtime and back down in the morning.'

'So you never told the police.'

'They never asked!'

'When did you get them back?'

'After the inquest. And I put them in the loft.'

'May we see them?'

'Well, I suppose it's a bit different now. I don't think Henry would mind. Why don't you come and get them?'

'Shall I ask my friend Jim to fetch them?' I didn't like to tell her I would find it very difficult to get to Devon to collect them.

'I'd rather it were you, dear. You were the last one to see him alive. And I'd rather have a woman crawling round the loft in my house than a man. It had better be you.'

'That might be a bit difficult, but I'll see what I can do.'

'Well, it's you or no one. I'll expect to hear from you again and you can tell me when you're coming. I'm here all the time. I don't go out a lot.'

Nor do I, I thought, but said to her, 'I'll speak to Jim and get back to you.'

'That's right. It will be good to meet you.'

We said our goodbyes and I sat there on the stairs thinking about a slightly feisty old lady who was stuck at home, and I compared her to myself. I decided it was high time I completely sorted out the agoraphobia and got on with my life. If only it were that easy! Meanwhile, I had a big problem. It was extremely unlikely that I could get to Gloria's house, and how would I cope if and when I did get there? I didn't think I could go clambering around in her loft. Or could I?

I phoned Jim that afternoon to tell him about this new development. I had to tell him twice before he took it in, and even then he questioned it.

'You say she hid information from the police? That's extraordinary. She may have had the evidence to have been able to establish he was murdered. Then she could have claimed his life insurance.'

I'd thought about that already. 'She was sure it was what Henry would have wanted. And she seems quite a determined lady.'

'But why would Henry want her to do that?'

'I suppose if something happened to him because what he was working on was dangerous, then she might have been in danger too if the police thought she knew.'

'It doesn't make a lot of sense. Although it does tell us one thing: he definitely didn't trust his colleagues.'

'So what happens to our plan of going to the police if we feel that we're getting close to danger?' A cold shiver ran up my spine.

'I don't know; we'll have to think about that one, although it won't be the same people in the Force nowadays. They'll be gone, or retired.'

'I thought you'd already spoken to the police. They told you the case was cut and dried and not to be reopened, didn't they?'

I thought I heard Jim mutter something, but then he spoke reassuringly. 'I didn't tell them we would be finding things out. I acted as if I totally agreed. We won't speak to them again until there's something concrete we can take to them. We'll cross that bridge when we come to it.'

Only a saying, I know, but I really wish he hadn't said 'bridge'. My thoughts went to the original 'suicide' victim, Dan Wallis.

'One more thing, Jim. Gloria said that Dan Wallis stretched his arms out sideways before then putting them forward to dive off the bridge.'

'That's really strange.'

'Do you think they were both hallucinating?'

'I think that is highly likely. But what made them hallucinate? Did someone give them drugs somehow?'

'Perhaps Gloria's papers will tell us.'

'Well, we'll have to get you to Gloria somehow, so that you can collect them, O Chosen One!'

I tried to laugh, but I was breathing too fast.

17

Somehow, by the end of the conversation, I had agreed with Jim to meet him the next day in the café by the Tube station. So on Wednesday, I managed to get out of the house in good time to walk up the street to meet him.

I pretended to pull up a weed or two before someone walked up the street outside my house. I quickly went through my gate and followed him. Not much of a distraction, but I tried to make it more of one by thinking about who he might be and where he was going, why he didn't have a briefcase or an umbrella, and why I had never seen him before, when I often sat at the small table in the window of my front room.

I stopped keeping pace with him as I began to wonder whether it was a coincidence that he had appeared soon after I had stepped out into the garden. Had he been watching out for me? Was he ready to follow me and then had to carry on past my house to avoid suspicion? I had reached the pillar box. I fumbled around in my bag as if I were looking for a letter and then pretended to post one. The mystery man carried on ahead of me, disappearing into a group of people near the station.

I took a deep breath to calm myself a little and carried on walking, telling myself that the man was only on his way to get a Tube. Probably he was a retired gentleman who didn't get out much. There was that phrase again – the one that defined me – the person who 'didn't get out much'. I preferred Gloria's view of me – a solver of mysteries.

By the time I reached the café shop, I was feeling slightly light-headed with the glory of the achievement. I was feeling silly, too. Who gets a high from walking such a short distance? But Jim's warm smile and his gentlemanly manners as he stood when I arrived made me think of nothing else but the fact that I was meeting a friend, in the way other people did.

The place was charming. The cream-coloured teacups with their lacy-edged saucers were exquisite, and the cakes arrived piled on cream-coloured, tiered cake plates. The tablecloths were sparkling white, and each place had been laid with crisp napkins in a serviette ring. It all looked very expensive. I wondered whether I should be paying or whether Jim would.

I thought we were there to talk about our findings, but when I started to say, 'Gloria told me...' Jim said, 'Not now,' and took a huge bite out of a slice of chocolate cake. I wondered if he was getting the heebie-jeebies as well. Or whether we were being watched, or perhaps he just wanted to enjoy the cake. I carefully sliced a mouthful of 'luscious lemon cake', and as I ate it I realised that this was a good experience, one not to be sullied by talk of suicide and intrigue.

'This is delicious, Jim. Thank you so much for discovering this place.'

'Well, now you know it's here, it will be good for you to come regularly for an afternoon cup of tea.'

I glanced at him. Was he trying to be funny? No, he was solemnly involved with eating that cake. Maybe he didn't realise what he had said.

'I'm not sure I can make it on my own.'

'You can; you did. I think you are magnificent to come this far, and the other day you went all the way to that other café up the road. You made that on your own.'

'Yes, but I didn't go in.'

'I'm not sure I would! But that's very different from this place. I think they will greet you like a friend in no time if you keep popping in for a cuppa.'

I glanced round the room. Certainly the lady who seemed to be in charge was spending a lot of time talking with the customers. While I looked she crouched down to talk to a baby in a pushchair, speaking to her by name. She had a lovely smile.

'I wonder if she's that baby's granny, or something?'

'I don't think so. I was here when they came in and the mum asked whether pushchairs were allowed. The owner, if that's who she is, not only said "yes" but rearranged most of the tables in the room to give the mum more space.'

With that, the person we were speaking about turned and came over to our table. 'Is everything all right for you? Would you like more water in the teapot? Or can I bring you more cakes?'

'No, thank you,' I said. 'The lemon cake lived up to its name: it was wonderful.'

'Well, thank you. I made that one myself! I don't make them all, but I do like to keep my hand in.'

'Who makes the chocolate cake?' asked Jim, having finally finished his mouthful.

'That's Ginny. She's an excellent cook, isn't she?'

We agreed, and she moved on to look after other customers.

'All right, you win. I could manage to come in and drink tea without you here. It is a lovely atmosphere.'

'And in next to no time it will be a home from home and you'll be here chatting with Trina every day.'

'How do you know her name? Did you know her already?'

'She's carrying a notebook to take the orders. It's got her name written on the front of it.'

'That's careless of her; any Tom, Dick or Harry could know her name.'

'Or Jim!' said Jim. My laughter stopped suddenly as I noticed a man in the shop beyond the café. The same man who I had thought was waiting to follow me.

'Jim, you're going to have to walk me home. I'm feeling a bit unsafe.'

'You can cope. You arrived here fine.'

'No, Jim, I don't think this is in my mind. I'll explain when we're in the house.'

'You are a woman of mystery. I'll pay the bill and we'll be on our way.'

As we left, I put my arm through Jim's. He looked a bit surprised but patted my hand. I gave him a grateful smile and kept pace with him as we walked back to my house.

Once in, I bolted the door behind Jim then walked through to the front room. I sat out of view watching the window.

Jim whispered, 'Am I being kidnapped or something?'

'No. I believe I was being followed up the road, but the man disappeared into the crowd by the Tube. But then came into the café shop.'

'What did he look like?'

'Brown mac, tallish, close-cropped hair.'

'Is that him?'

It was. We watched him go down the road.

'Quick,' said Jim, 'say goodbye to me on the step and I'll see where he goes.'

We went to the door.

'Bye, dear,' said Jim, then carefully pecked me on the cheek as if we had known each other for ages.

He gave me a quick wave as he went through the gate, then turned left to go down the road in the direction the brown-mackintoshed gentleman had gone. I shut the door and bolted it, then went to sit by my window, watching for him to return. My cheek felt warm and cherished, but the rest of me was racked with worry.

18

Jim was gone for about twenty minutes. During that time I alternated between walking around the room trying to concentrate on tidying the odd cushion or anything else that I could possibly construe as being out of place, and going upstairs to peer out of the bedroom window. I tried praying. I couldn't calm myself. I had become quite convinced that something terrible had happened to him. Then I saw him walking slowly back up the road towards my house.

I rushed to the front door and pulled him in. 'What happened? You've been ages.'

'Everything's fine,' said Jim, smiling broadly as he took off his coat and looped it over my banisters. 'No need to worry.'

I followed him into my sitting room, feeling that he was taking liberties but nevertheless desperate to know what had happened. He sat himself on my sofa and stretched his legs out in front of him. I perched on the edge of the easy chair while he looked at me, saying nothing. I was beginning to get mad with him. Why wouldn't the man tell me?

'Our mystery man is nothing more than an old romantic.'

'What do you mean by that, Jim? Stop talking in riddles, please.'

'I followed him to the corner where he turned into Travis Road. I then followed him all the way up there. I got out my street map and paused several times to look at it because he was dawdling a bit. It wasn't really a map, but a train timetable, but hopefully it looked like a map.'

'Just tell me,' I said.

'Okay. He kept slowing up and turned round once. So I walked back to the corner as if I were checking the road sign.'

'So where was he going?'

'I'm getting there. He went up to the second turning and into the close – what's that road called? Williams Close, I think. But the road sign hasn't got an apostrophe and I really think it should have one.'

'Are you going to tell me what he was doing?'

Jim smiled, a teasing, enigmatic smile. 'Guess!'

'How can I guess? I haven't a clue!'

'I'll give you one. Under his mac he had something to give to someone. He probably felt silly carrying it, or he didn't want anyone to see.'

I gave Jim a look which I hoped showed him that I was becoming even more annoyed.

'Okay,' he said. 'I'll tell you. From under his mac he produced a bouquet of red roses. He walked up to a front door in the close and he knocked. It was some time before the door was opened, but luckily he was too busy fidgeting about to notice me. The door opened and a woman looked out. She didn't seem to be too pleased to see him, but he gave her the roses and talked quietly to her, and she let him in the door.'

'Oh. So he was a man buying roses for his girlfriend.'

'Yes. That's the extent of the mystery. I should think he came in the gift shop to find something else as well, but didn't see anything to buy.'

I felt strangely deflated and not a little stupid. I had made Jim walk back with me for nothing and taken his arm to pretend we were a couple. Jim was watching me, a smile playing on his lips. I tried to ignore him.

'Let's have a cuppa,' he said. 'I can put the kettle on, if you like.'

'No, I'll do it. I'm the one who's made a fool of herself. Sorry it was about nothing.'

'Don't be silly. We have got to be alert; we have no idea if we're getting into anything sinister. Anyway, it was all rather fun, following someone and having to pretend I always walked up side roads. Mind you,' he smiled and raised his eyebrows, 'if he spots me coming out of your house then he'll probably realise he was being followed by someone pretending to read a map and he'll become curious about it.'

'Then he'll start following us to see what *we're* up to, I suppose! I'm going to make some tea to stop this nonsense.'

'Yes, please do, because we need to talk, and I shall have to be going soon or my brother-in-law will be wondering where I've got to. It's one of those households where the evening meal is always at six o'clock and no one can be late.'

So over a cup of tea – no eats this time, Jim was too full of cake – we discussed how I was going to get to Gloria. We agreed I couldn't at the moment but I could manage to maybe walk to the café each day and step up my programme of working on my agoraphobia.

Jim suddenly scrambled to his feet. 'Jenny, I must go. Look at the time! I'll ring you tomorrow.'

I went to the door to see him out, and as he went he pecked me on the cheek again. Only this time, I think he really wanted to; it wasn't play-acting. It surprised me, but it pleased me too. I watched him as he walked back to the station, turning once to wave goodbye.

Being with Jim had been exhilarating and interesting, but it tired me out. I sunk into my favourite deep chair, simply appreciating being on my own. It was all very well working on the mystery with Jim, but solitude was what I was used to. I seemed to be on some sort of roundabout that I was not able to stop.

Over the next few days, Jim phoned me every day, even if he didn't have an update. He always started talking about the investigation, as we now both called it, but quickly seemed to lapse into chit-chat. At first I was flattered. But he was becoming a little like a therapist. He seemed absolutely set on encouraging me to walk to the café each day.

'Have you been? How was it? Did you meet anyone to chat to?'

I went twice and spoke to no one apart from ordering my coffee. On the third occasion, the owner of the café, Trina, stopped at my table and asked me what I was reading. We found we had similar tastes, but she had read all John Grisham's books except for the one I was reading, *The Client.*

'It's quite an early one; did you miss it?' I asked.

'I only buy books from charity shops, so I haven't seen a copy. I love charity shops, don't you?'

The narrowness of my life crowded into my mind. The very thought of going into a charity shop terrified me, although part of my brain reasoned that in fact once I were there, all would be fine and I could browse like everyone else. I remembered doing that with my mother when she was well, but the stuffy smell of the shop had stifled me.

Trina was wiping the adjacent table while she waited for my reply.

'I haven't actually been in a charity shop for years. I went in one that really smelled bad and it rather put me off. So I've missed out on bargains.'

'My favourite is the shop up the road. It is rather good in there; I think they wash everything.'

'Perhaps not the books!'

She laughed. 'No, but they always seem pretty clean! They probably chuck out the ones with grubby pages or dusty covers! Is your chap a reader?'

'My chap?'

'The bloke you met when you first came here.'

'Jim? I don't know. We haven't known each other long.'

'Ah.' She gave me a sideways look – that's the only way I could describe it. Somehow it was full of meaning. If I had known her better I would have asked why she looked at me like that, but I thought I knew. Probably in her mind I was an adulteress meeting a married man, although there was nothing untoward that happened here in the café – or anywhere, for that matter.

She spoke again. 'He seemed lovely. You should keep hold of that one!'

I smiled.

But something had changed. If people thought that Jim and I were a couple, in any sense of the word, then I had to make up my mind whether to pull back or keep seeing him. Part of me knew that my anxiety was feeding my thoughts: I felt trapped in a situation I couldn't control.

I tried to reason things out. Keeping things 'professional' was certainly not on Jim's agenda. It was only a friendship, but talking to him brought back the laughter in my life. I was taking risks now, even with people like Trina, when I began to joke with her. A few months earlier I would have perhaps smiled and returned to my book. No... a few months earlier I wouldn't have been in the café at all. I didn't know what to think.

One week after our joint visit to the café, Jim phoned to say his holiday was nearly over and he would be returning to Devon the next day with Stephen.

'I wondered if we could meet again before I go, and sort out our plans.'

Feeling spooked by the conversation with Trina, I asked, 'What plans?'

'I don't know. But Gloria is expecting to hear from you and we need to know how to respond to that when you're ready. I was wondering if you'd be able to spend time with your aunt again, and maybe we could visit Gloria together.'

I sighed with relief. I was not ready to talk about any more personal plans. I didn't want to meet in the café, though. Trina would comment about it afterwards.

'Why don't you come here? It will be more private to talk.'

As soon as I said it, I wondered if he might misconstrue it. But it was all right. He said, 'Thank you, that would be most kind. I need to be back to collect Stephen by one o'clock, so would it be possible to meet at about ten tomorrow? Or is that too early?'

'That's absolutely fine. I'll see you at ten-ish.' I resisted the urge to encourage him to bring Stephen. That would really complicate matters.

'Wonderful. I won't be late. But look out for me and open the door quickly in case that gent from up the road is watching!'

I laughed. 'I think he was making up after a quarrel with his girlfriend, and I am neurotic.'

'No you're not. I think we're right to be a little cautious.'

Although I was unsure about Jim, it was exciting to have someone coming to see me again. I wondered if I would ever get over the pure pleasure of entertaining. I baked some biscuits and checked my supply of ground coffee. It smelled okay, although I never used it when I was on my own. I had to hunt for the cafétiere: it had been pushed to the back of the shelf. I gave it a good wash.

I was up early the next morning to scoot round with the vacuum cleaner and find all my papers and bits ready for our discussion. I felt strangely nervous. Everything was ready on the tray and I had boiled the kettle by 9.45, when there was a ring on the doorbell. When I opened it, there was Jim with a huge bouquet of flowers.

'Mystery man isn't the only one who can buy a bunch of flowers,' said Jim as he passed them to me.

I felt the heat rise to my face. 'Well, thank you, Jim. I'll find a vase. How kind.'

I walked through to the kitchen, leaving him standing in the hall. The flowers were mostly white and purple-ish, like huge daisies. They looked beautiful. Jim followed me through to the kitchen, so there was no disguising the fact that I had blushed.

'Wow – what's this? Home-made biscuits?'

'Yes, I didn't have any shop ones.' It sounded pathetic, as if shop-bought ones were better. Why couldn't I graciously accept a compliment?

Jim's boyish grin made me even more disconcerted. 'I love biscuits, especially home-made ones,' he said.

He noticed the cafétiere. 'Ah, do you mind if I have tea?'

'No, that's fine. I merely wanted to give you choice.'

The teapot was ready for exactly that purpose, so I made us both tea while Jim watched.

'You take the tray, Jim, and I'll pop the flowers into water.'

It took me a few minutes to locate a vase, which proved to be too small. In the end I used a large white jug and carried the resulting display into my sitting room and placed it on the small table by the hearth. I saw that Jim had put another log on the fire. I felt slightly wrong-footed, unsure that a visitor should carry out that task. I wished I had used the small electric heater instead.

I poured the tea while Jim talked about timescales for visiting Gloria. It all seemed too sudden for me.

'I don't know, Jim. I don't think I can do it.'

'You managed Devon before; you can surely drive down again!'

'I had my aunt with me and it was an emergency.'

'She would have managed without you. You probably told yourself it was an emergency to make yourself get there. This is a different kind of emergency. Why not give it a try?'

'I'm not sure you understand how difficult it is.'

'I'm trying to. Is there anything I can do to help?'

There was silence for a bit. I could think of loads of things to say, but they weren't appropriate. *Just go away and leave me alone. Come and get me and take me there yourself. You do it, or get a friend to pretend to be me. Bring Gloria and her papers here. Stop putting pressure on me.* All I could say was, 'I'm a hopeless case. I don't think anyone can help. You'd better go.'

Jim put down his tea. He began to gather together his papers. He wasn't looking at me; in fact, he was looking anywhere but at me. I was trying not to let out the tears that were forming in my eyes. I felt desolate.

'I'm sorry, Jim,' I managed to mutter.

Jim shrugged. 'For the record, I don't think you're hopeless. I was genuinely asking if I could help, and I would really like to. You have a fine brain, Jenny, you're a lovely lady and I love your sense of humour and the way you think of others when you're struggling yourself. But if you want to be left alone, I will respect that.'

Before I could think of anything to say, he had grabbed his coat and gone.

19

I felt hopeless. No longer was I working on the mystery – I had ground to a halt. I wasn't hearing from Jim and I didn't feel I deserved to hear from him ever again.

It took me three days to make myself walk to the café to have a coffee. I'd finished rereading *The Client* and I wanted to lend it to Trina. That was one good thing about the whole Jim episode: I had managed to go further without panicking and now had somewhere, someone, to walk towards.

The place was empty of customers when I arrived, and Trina greeted me like an old friend. 'Jenny, lovely to see you again today. The table near the window is for you, unless you'd rather sit in your usual place?'

I realised I had a usual place! I hadn't thought about it before, but somehow I had always found the table in the corner where I had first sat with Jim. It occurred to me that Trina might want me in the window seat because an empty café looks a bit uninviting. I followed her suggestion, but sat to look into the shop. I felt less exposed that way.

'Are you having your usual?' asked Trina. Another 'usual'; surprising how they cropped up without really being invited.

'Yes, thank you.' I waited for my cappuccino to arrive. I missed Jim dreadfully in this place. I hadn't really felt like that at home – but this was where we had begun to get to know each other. Now it was the place to feel lonely.

I looked round at the café and into the shop beyond. I thought of the mystery man who was trying to find something for his girlfriend. I came to the conclusion that I knew nothing at all about relationships and probably never would. Two couples had come into the shop area, each looking at small homely items. One of the men laughed softly while turning to smile at his lady. I felt so left out. Would I ever have an intimate relationship, or even a close friend?

Trina put my coffee in front of me. 'You all right, love? You look a bit down in the dumps today. Your man hasn't left you, has he?'

I battled to stop the tears from welling up. I couldn't believe it; here I was, at my age, behaving like a teenager. 'I think I've upset him, that's all.'

'Men – they're always getting the grumps. Best thing, pretend it's your fault and say sorry and then he'll say sorry and job's done. It'll all be hunky-dory again. And if it's really important, whatever's got between you, it can be sorted out later!'

I blotted at my face with a tissue, in as offhand a manner as I could. 'I didn't realise it mattered until I just told you about it.'

'Well, give him a ring and sort it out, then.'

One of the couples had drifted from the shop into the café.

'I'd best go, dear. We'll talk later.' Trina walked off to see to her customers. I could see now that they had turned round that they were expecting a baby. That part of my life had gone, I knew, but I didn't envy them. How would I know how to look after a baby?

I imagined Jim with children. I couldn't even remember how many nieces and nephews he had. I knew Stephen was his sister's son and she had two girls as well. Did I know if he had other brothers and sisters? I could ring and ask him, but that would be a bit odd, really. Was Trina right, suggesting I should make the first move? I didn't know. Still, I *had* rather given him the brush-off, even if I were to say sorry.

I started to imagine a few scenarios of what might happen if I were to ring. The worst possible was that he would tell me to get lost. Even as I thought it, I realised that would be no worse than how I felt now. The best case scenario would be that he would be his usual lovely self. Unlikely, because I had obviously hurt him. I tried to imagine what my psychologist would say and knew without a doubt that he would tell me to ring Jim. Well, not exactly tell me, but help me to come to the right conclusion. I finished my cappuccino quickly and got up to go.

My handbag felt heavy – I remembered that I still had the book I was going to lend to Trina. She was busy serving, so I didn't disturb her. She looked up as I passed. 'Off already?'

'Yes, I need to go and make a phone call.'

She smiled and turned back to her customers. I put the money for the coffee by the till and hurried out of the shop and back home. I wished I had a mobile phone to ring Jim straight away. I had been so housebound for so long that I had never even been to look at any.

I distracted myself on the way home by mentally rehearsing what I would say when I rang Jim. But once I arrived home, my resolve frittered away. My head became full of half-remembered conversations: 'Give him a ring and sort it out then'; 'Mystery man isn't the only one who can buy flowers'; 'You should keep hold of that one'; 'Is there anything I can do to help?'; 'You'd better go.' How could I be so cruel to such a lovely man?

I took a few long, slow breaths, calmed my thoughts, then picked up the phone and dialled his Devon number. He answered straight away.

'Hello, Jim. Jenny here.'

There was a pause before he said, in a very bright voice, 'Hello, Jenny, what can I do for you?'

'Forgive me.' As soon as I said it I began to worry that this was not the way to speak to Jim and he would think I was pathetic.

'No, you forgive me. I shouldn't have left like that. We should have talked longer so that I could understand better.'

'But I should have tried to explain. I'm sorry.'

Jim laughed – a huge laugh that sounded like it came from his whole body. 'Stop and think about what we're saying, Jenny. We are trying to outdo each other with our sorriness!'

I was laughing too, totally relieved that it had all been so easy.

'Jenny, can I ring you later? I'm a bit tied up here at the moment and I have so much I want to say to you.'

'Yes – I'm not going anywhere.'

'That's good, if you know what I mean. I shall look forward to talking to you soon.'

'Me too. Bye Jim, for now.'

'Goodbye, dear. Take care.'

I sat on my stairs cradling the phone. There was no avoiding it. I was developing strong feelings for Jim. I really hoped I wasn't deluding myself that he seemed to like me too. It had been lovely taking his arm the other day and feeling how steady he was. But I must be careful not to get carried away by my feelings, and remain firmly sensible.

I closed my eyes and thought about how exactly he had said 'dear'. It made me feel special, however he intended it to sound.

Over lunch, it dawned on me that relinking with Jim rather meant I was 'back on the case'. What could I do about Gloria? If I phoned her and told her about the agoraphobia, she may feel very guilty about what Henry had done. *Did* she feel guilty? Maybe not; after all, she was convinced that even though he jumped off the cliff, it was not his own choice. So not suicide. Maybe it would be all right to explain. I made a note to ask Jim what he thought.

I started to think about Gloria living with this all those years. She must have struggled to keep it true in her mind that it was not suicide. She had convinced their son, or maybe he was convinced anyway because he knew the kind of dad he was. A father like my own father, maybe. A man who carried me on his shoulders and invented great stories to keep me amused. I deliberately turned my mind away from the day I saw Henry jump – it always popped into my mind when I remembered being on my father's shoulders, although I'd had many rides up there before and since.

Another possibility was to try to persuade her that Jim was a lovely, safe man and he would be quite all right climbing into the loft – in fact, better than me. Perhaps my thoughts about Jim taking a female friend to help him were not so outrageous.

Imagining Jim having another female friend was rather uncomfortable; in fact, disturbing. I began to pace around the house, desperate for him to ring me back. When did he say he'd ring? I tried to remember whether he had given a time. And what was he doing that was so important? I reasoned with myself to calm my fears that he had other pressing engagements and was meeting loads of people whom he valued much more than me. I gave up thinking about it all and went to clean the kitchen. Not that it really needed it; it was easy to keep the place clean when I was home so much and only had myself to think about.

By mid-afternoon I had decided that in fact Jim had no intention of ringing at all and I had made a great mistake saying that I wasn't going anywhere. For the first time for many years, I really wanted to go out of the house. Maybe this was because I had to wait in and wasn't choosing to stay at home. I was desperate to walk up the road to have another coffee in the café and talk to Trina again.

Jim rang when I had my hand on the front door ready to go. 'I was on my way out,' I said.

'Oh, I'm sorry. I thought you said you'd be in all day.'

'Something's changing. I really wanted to go and have a coffee up the road before the café closed.'

'That's great news. Well, don't let me stop you!'

'No, I want to talk to you… You've been busy today; what have you been up to?'

'Sorting out Stephen. He's not happy on his training scheme so I've been to the college to see if there is anything with more time on the work element that he can do. Options are very limited, though.'

'Did they suggest anything?'

'No, but his tutor, a lovely lady, helped Stephen understand he should stay on the basic life skills course. The trouble is, he knows it all because I have taught him. His tutor suggested that he would be very useful in helping her to show others how to do things. Stephen was thrilled to think he would be like an assistant.'

'She sounds good.'

'Yes, she is. If he can get through this year he will move on to better things. He is one of the few who will be able to hold down a mainstream job, albeit quite basic. He is already managing a couple of days a week in the supermarket, and in the summer he did pretty well helping me in the café. He's very polite to the customers. He's not good at taking orders, though – his writing isn't quite up to it – but he will carry out the food and put chairs in, wipe tables, that sort of thing.'

'It's good that you've been able to give him the opportunity.'

'Yes, as long as I have The Beachfarer, I'll be able to give him some employment. It's moving on from there that's the problem. I won't have the café forever.'

I realised that we had lapsed into quite personal chat, even though it was about his 'son'. I felt comfortable talking about him, although my knowledge was minimal. I was careful not to make out I knew more than I did.

I thought it was time to change the subject. 'Jim, we need to talk about Gloria.'

'Oh dear.'

'Why "oh dear"?'

'Well, wasn't that what we fell out over before? I was too pushy or something.'

'I was too negative.'

'Do you know what you would like to do now?'

I told Jim my thoughts and asked him what he would do.

'Ringing Gloria is a good idea. I don't think she'll have me in the house; she wasn't even keen on talking to me over the phone. I don't have a female friend to take with me to see her, even if they did pretend they were you.'

'Oh no, I wouldn't expect them to do that. It would be totally wrong. Anyway, Gloria knows my voice.'

Jim laughed. 'So it's okay for us to pretend we're a couple in case mystery man turns round, but not to pretend in any other way?'

'What do you mean?'

'The other day, when you took my arm.'

'No, not that bit.' I didn't dare say anything else. There was a pause.

'Have I come to the wrong conclusions?' asked Jim.

The air around me suddenly felt charged. I wished Jim was there so that we could look at each other and I didn't have to say anything. All I could say was, 'Possibly. But let's get back to talking about Gloria.'

Jim was laughing again. 'Jenny, you are a one. All right, we'll talk about Gloria on condition that we talk about *us* next time we meet.'

I felt warm and smug at the thought of an 'us'. 'Good idea,' I said.

The upshot of our discussion was that I should talk to Gloria again and tell her about my anxiety difficulties as fully as I could. I felt empowered to do that with Jim backing me up. I would suggest to her that Jim should go on his own to collect the box file. If she were not happy with that, I would discuss the possibility of her waiting for me to be able to get there.

'She's in her nineties. Is she in good health?' asked Jim.

'I'd better find out.'

But even as we rung off and said our goodbyes, the doubts set in. Would I manage to speak to Gloria? And would she refuse point-blank to let Jim go? It might be years before I was ready; could I get there in time?

20

When Jim and I finished the phone call, I procrastinated. There's no other word for it. I decided it would be teatime for Gloria, without having the faintest idea about her routine. I thought I had better write things down to say to her, in case I got it wrong. I had scribbles of notes in front of me, so there was no need. Then I decided I should have my meal first, but while I was cooking I got it into my head that Jim would ring to see what she said before I had even managed to speak to her.

I was passing through the hall, still undecided as to what to do, when the phone rang. I picked it up, expecting it to be Jim. But it was a stranger's voice that asked for Jenny Drake.

'Yes, Jenny Drake speaking,' I said.

'Hello, good to talk to you. It's Freddie Standish here. I hope you don't mind me ringing you, but my mother said you called her about my father's death.'

As I replied, I tried to work out whether he was thinking I'd done something wrong. 'Yes, I did. I hope I didn't upset her. Did she tell you why I rang?'

It was then I realised this man had no Devonshire accent. I felt my whole body stiffen as I listened to him speak again. 'Oh yes, she said you were six years old when you witnessed him jumping of the cliff and that he crossed himself.'

I took myself in hand. This must be Freddie: how else would he know about my conversation with Gloria? He must be genuine. I tried to concentrate as he told me he was staying in Islington for a few days before flying from Heathrow on a business conference. He added, 'So would it be possible for me to pop round and see you before I go? I'd really like to hear what happened, as far as you can remember it.'

My hackles rose. There was a pause before I answered, 'Couldn't we discuss this over the phone now?'

'Well, yes we could, but I have so many questions I thought it would be good to meet. Anyway, Mother said that it can't have been easy for you, so I wanted to make sure I didn't upset you.'

I was unsure. 'Let me think about it. Ring me this evening.'

'Certainly. I'll do that.'

As soon as we'd finished the call, I rang Jim. 'I've had a phone call from Freddie Standish. He wants to come to talk to me about his father's death.'

'Did you check he is who he says he is?' asked Jim. He sounded a little worried.

'He seemed to know exactly what I had told his mother. He sounded genuine; in fact, he sounded a bit concerned about me.'

Jim took me through the whole conversation. Finally he said, 'You know, he does sound genuine. If you've told no one else apart from me about your conversation with Gloria, then he could only know from Gloria herself.'

I felt a little more confident. 'Do you think it would be okay to meet him here? I know I can get to the café, but that's only when I haven't got the added uncertainty of meeting someone I don't know.'

'When I met Freddie he told me he is a lay preacher,' said Jim. 'If you're sure who he is, then he'd be a safe person to have in the house, I expect.'

Feeling reassured, I was happy to talk to Freddie again. I reasoned with myself that I had coped with Jim coming to the house, so I could certainly cope with someone Jim had already met.

When Freddie rang back, he sounded warm and friendly. He was delighted he could meet with me, and he so wanted to talk to someone about his dad. Somehow, by the time the conversation with Freddie was over, I had invited him for coffee the next morning. I had no choice, really; Freddie had to be at Heathrow by two o'clock for his flight.

After our conversation, I went straight into the kitchen to bake some scones. I really hoped lay preachers didn't go visiting and get given so many scones that they hated them!

The next morning, I was ready in good time. Freddie arrived on the doorstep at exactly ten o'clock. He wiped his feet on the outside mat, taking my hand and shaking it firmly as he introduced himself. He was a tall, thin, bespectacled man. He didn't look as I had imagined. He was older than I expected, but then, of course, considering his mother's age, it was probable that he was well into his sixties or even older.

He shrugged off his black coat and hung it over the end of the banisters without me even inviting him to. His height seemed to fill the room. I felt anxious but he was clearly trying to put me at ease.

'Charming place you have here, Miss Drake. Lovely. I should think you find it very handy living here for getting to the shows and museums.'

'Yes, it is handy for those things. Although I don't go out very much.'

'Why's that, then? Oh, sorry, I shouldn't pry.'

I offered him a cup of tea and went through to the kitchen. I had arranged the stack of home-made scones earlier and they looked good. My scones didn't always rise and I usually made very small quantities, it only being me. This time I had made a large batch. I wondered if Freddie would eat many; they could go in the freezer otherwise.

I had delayed long enough. I brought through the steaming tea. Freddie seemed really pleased to see the scones. 'I remember my mother's scones: they were really good. But she doesn't make them these days. In fact, she hardly ever does any baking. Her daily takes her a hot meal twice a week but otherwise she does herself eggs or cheese on toast, that sort of thing.'

'Do you see her often?'

'It's a bit difficult these days. I'm so busy – just off to Bulgaria... But we have a grand time when we are together. She doesn't travel to Leeds to stay with us any more.'

We didn't seem to get to Henry's death for ages. When I finally approached the subject, Freddie said, 'You know, Miss Drake, my father was a man of secrets. My mother is

126

quite convinced that he didn't commit suicide, mostly because he'd said he'd cook the evening meal.'

I nodded. I wondered whether to say there was more to it than that, but thought not.

Freddie continued, 'I know he said that, but I think maybe he had a big secret that is best left alone. There was a strange woman at the funeral. I didn't ever discover who she was. That's something you might want to find out about, but I don't think it's worth it. Sometimes family secrets are best hidden. I've never said anything to my mother, so I trust you will keep that from her.'

'Of course I will. I'd hate her to be upset.'

'Me too, of course. In fact, it might be better if she didn't know I had come to talk to you. I really don't want her to worry and make her think more about the suicide. It's bad enough that she doesn't accept the facts. I just listen to her theories about Dad's death, whatever she says.'

'She thinks you agree with her.'

'I did as a child. I was very, very sad and angry. But as an adult the feeling that there had been foul play merely disappeared. I realised that some things happen in life that are better unexplained.'

'I know what you mean.' I was thinking of my own problems with walking down the road, which hadn't improved much since that day on the beach. All I had achieved recently was meeting Jim. I briefly wondered whether it would have been better if I had never known about Jim's suspicions regarding Henry's death.

As if reading my thoughts, Freddie went on, 'Your friend Jim is causing some unrest in the area. It might be best if he let it all drop as well. I really don't want another public investigation. It would kill my mother.'

I kept quiet. Jim was not the sort of person to create any unpleasantness. Not only was I confused, I was also wondering why Freddie was so unaccepting of his mother's wish to find out what had led to his father's death. Maybe he was in denial.

'I hadn't realised Jim was causing trouble. Your mother sounded so pleased that we were interested in what happened to your father.'

'No criticism of you and your friend, Miss Drake, but she is ninety-two and rather a frail old lady.'

Now I felt terrible. Had I unwittingly worried an old lady? If Freddie thought so, then maybe I had. 'I'm sorry, we didn't want to cause any upset.'

'And I don't want to cause any for you,' said Freddie. 'If you ever want to talk things through, ring me, and preferably not my mother.'

With that he stood up. He turned to go, setting the lampshade swaying slightly as it touched the top of his balding head. I shuddered. I felt really uncomfortable but couldn't work out why. I was pleased he left really quickly. He didn't seem at all like the person Jim had described. I couldn't understand it.

When he had gone, I carefully bagged up the few remaining scones and put them in the freezer for another day. I popped my cold cup of tea in the microwave to reheat. As I did so, I realised he hadn't asked me about what I had seen as a small child. He had come with his own agenda, which certainly wasn't to go through his father's last actions. I felt so uneasy about the visit that I stopped the microwave and poured away my drink. I tipped away the milk in the jug, and poured the sugar into the bin. I even took the uneaten scones out of the freezer and threw them away.

Then I felt very silly and overdramatic. But I certainly wasn't sure about keeping quiet about his visit. Nor about stopping our investigation. On thinking about it, I didn't believe I had upset Gloria at all.

I would have to talk to Jim.

21

The uneasy feeling stayed with me. I tried to get hold of Jim, but there was no reply to my phone calls. I sat on the stairs by the phone, thinking about the situation. Despite Freddie's caution about contacting his mother, I felt really strongly that I had to speak to Gloria again. I needed to tell her I wouldn't be collecting that box file. Anyway, I had promised Jim I would ring her. I would be very careful not to upset her, and this could be the last call.

I took myself in hand and made the call. My heart was pounding as I waited for her to answer. When she did pick up the phone, I felt so anxious that I could hardly tell her who was calling.

'Oh, hello, Jenny. You're the lady who doesn't think Henry took his own life, aren't you?'

Her voice didn't sound quite like it did before. I was concerned. 'Yes, I am. Are you all right?'

'I have a cold, dear. Might be bronchitis; it was last time.' She coughed. It didn't sound too good at all.

'Are you well enough to talk?'

'Yes, yes. Best get this stuff out of my house. Don't want to pop my clogs before you collect it. When are you coming?'

'I don't know if it will be soon.' She was coughing again, so I waited until she stopped, then I carried on. 'I was phoning to tell you that I have real problems getting out of the house.'

'Disabled are you, dear?'

'Well, no. Not in the usual sense. I have agoraphobia.'

'What's that? Fear of going out, isn't it?'

'Yes.' I felt flat and exposed.

'I don't want your friend coming on his own. Couldn't you come with him?' I could hear Gloria's breathing was heavy and wheezy. This wasn't the time to give her a definite 'no' to the visit.

'Don't worry about it. I'll see what I can do. But you had better see the doctor. Soon.'

'I know, I know. But he'll only put me in the hospital again. Or start talking about me going into a home. Not having that. But there's no one to look after me here.'

'Do you have a neighbour who can pop in?'

'She's nearly as old as me. No, I'll soldier on. But don't you be too long in getting here.'

'Is there anyone else you see during the week?'

'Usually my cleaner comes in but she's been off somewhere with her grandchildren.'

'What about your son?'

'Oh, I don't want to worry him. He's got his own life to lead. Anyway, I think he's in Germany talking at some conference.'

I didn't correct her. Freddie must have had his reasons for not telling her exactly where he was going. 'I expect he'd like to know you're not well.'

'It's only a cold, dear. Don't fuss. I'll be fine.' She was seized by a spasm of coughing again.

'Freddie popped in to see me today, and said he was concerned about you.'

'Really, dear? That's strange. I thought he had gone to Germany already.'

'He was on his way to the airport. He stopped by and he enjoyed some scones and a cup of tea. He wanted to talk things through.'

Gloria had begun coughing again as I spoke. She seemed to be heaving for breath. Maybe I was distressing her?

'I'd better go; talking is making your cough worse.'

'Yes, dear. Take care.'

'And promise me you'll see a doctor!'

'Yes, dear.'

I was worried. She sounded really ill. She needed someone to check up on her. It occurred to me that if I managed to catch Freddie before he flew, he might come back. At least this would resolve how to get the box file to Jim. Although he might be so concerned about his mother that he wouldn't have a chance to look for it. I became angry with myself for even thinking about the papers when Gloria was ill, then angry with the agoraphobia that made me virtually disabled. Angry that I couldn't sort myself out. I rang Jim and outlined the situation.

'I don't know what to do – she sounds really ill,' I told him.

'I've got her son's number. Shall I ring him?'

'He's flying to Bulgaria. Should we stop him?'

'Bulgaria? When I met him in the pub, I thought he said his next trip was to Germany.'

'That's what Gloria thought. Maybe his plans changed.'

'Probably. Anyway, I don't have a mobile number. I could try talking to his answerphone, in case anyone listens to his messages for him. Someone needs to take care of her. What would your aunt do if she were ill? She lives on her own, doesn't she?'

'She's involved in church and WI, that sort of stuff. One of her friends would pop round if she were ill, I'm sure. And her neighbour has my number.'

'Doesn't sound as if Gloria has that sort of network.'

'She seems very alone. If I were living nearby, I'd probably try to get her some help, or at least get her to see the doctor.'

'Well, come. Yes, you must come. I could get to you on the train tomorrow morning and you could drive me back. You drove your aunt back in an emergency, didn't you?'

'I had to hire a car. I don't have one.'

'Oh, I didn't know that.'

The thought of going to Devon was at once horrifying and alluring. I loved Devon, having grown up there. Could I do that – drive down with Jim as a passenger? I had money to hire a car.

'I might be able to hire a car again, if you could come to make the journey with me. You'd have to be here in time to help me go to pick it up. It's further than I usually go.'

'Well done, Jenny. Conquering your fears to rescue an old lady. I'll see if I can sort something out for Stephen and ring you back to tell you what I'm doing. Bye for now.'

I put the phone down. I was smiling at his enthusiasm. But then fear crept through my body like a sliver of ice. I began to shake and cry.

22

I fought the fear by getting back to domestic tasks, my normal standby. I finished cooking my tea but had no appetite for it. I covered it and put it in the fridge. I really wanted to talk to Mike – I needed support, or reassurance, or something, but most of all I hoped he would say I mustn't go. It was good that it was out of hours, or I would have rung him.

I managed to eat yoghurt, which sat heavily in my stomach. I made myself a cup of tea and put a lot of sugar in it. It was disgusting, but I made myself drink it, then poured myself another. I couldn't think what to do. At least when Aunt Judy had needed to be taken home, it was an emergency, and I was the only one who could sort it out. I remembered what Jim said about that. Had I thought of it as an emergency so that I could manage to go? I didn't think so, but how would I know?

I found the phone number of the car hire firm. I had no idea if they had long opening hours, and I couldn't book the car anyway until I knew when Jim was coming. I wondered if he alone could be the named driver. It might be easier if I were the passenger. The more I thought about it, the less sure I was. Driving would keep me focused and busy.

By the time Jim phoned, I had decided the whole thing was ridiculous and no way could I drive to Devon.

'I've decided I can't do it,' I blurted out, as soon as I was sure it was him.

'Jenny, you can. I will help you. I've sorted out a friend to keep an eye on Stephen for the day while I come to accompany you, and I've phoned Gloria's son.'

'Well, we won't be needed then, so I've no need to do it.'

'On the contrary. Her son *is* in Germany, but his wife gave me his number. She's flying out tonight to join him. She has a seminar to run. All she could do to help was to phone Gloria and urge her to see the doctor.'

'So is Gloria agreeing to see the doctor?'

'No. She says she's found some old medicine in the cupboard from last time and she's taking that.'

'I think it needs penicillin. She didn't sound at all good.'

'That's what Freddie said. He rang her from Germany, then rang me back. He's really keen that we go and try to persuade her to get some help. Especially you – he says she respects a woman's opinion on a matter of health.'

'But Jim, I don't know if I can do it.'

'I'll be there beside you. I can even drive, if you like.'

'I don't know. Sometimes I'm better with distractions.'

'Look, you hire the car to be picked up tomorrow at two o'clock with both our names to drive. I'll be with you by one-ish and we'll sort out the driving as we go along. We can do this together, Jenny. Let's at least try. We could always turn around if you're really spooked.'

There was something about Jim that made me more confident. Reluctantly, I agreed.

'I'm holding you to that, Jenny, because I know you can do it.'

I rang the car hire company at about eight o'clock; I couldn't make myself do it before then. I fully expected that there would be no one there, but someone answered and very quickly and smoothly booked me a Mini. The only problem came when I tried to put Jim on as a second driver – I didn't know enough about him. I didn't even know his address.

'Well, you sort it out when you come in, love. Two o'clock will be fine.'

I spent the evening filling a bag with a few things for two or three days in Devon. I couldn't decide what to take. I put in ordinary day clothes, then decided to add a really good dress. A little out of date, but I hadn't been to the shops for years. I had some pearls but otherwise I took some beads that would go with everything, and one or two scarves. I remembered pyjamas, but it was only when I was putting them in the bag that I realised I hadn't rung Aunt Judy to invite myself to stay.

My aunt picked up the phone with a cheerful, 'Judy Harris here, how can I help you?'

'Hi Aunt Judy, it's Jenny. How would it be if I came for a couple of days to stay?'

'Wonderful, wonderful. Haven't seen you since you brought me back from our grand capital city. Yes, you know I'll always have space for you. When are you coming?'

'Would tomorrow be all right?'

'Tomorrow? That's a bit soon. How about next week?'

'No, it has to be tomorrow. I have an appointment to go to. But don't worry, I can always book into somewhere.'

'No, no, of course you can come. But you'll have to make up your own bed. Lisa doesn't come until Friday.'

'That's no problem. I certainly won't mind doing that.'

'Well, I'll have some lunch ready for you, then.'

'No, don't do that. I won't be there until the evening, and I will have already had a meal.' I didn't like to think of her making a meal especially for me. If I didn't get to eat tomorrow, I would have to go without.

'Well, that's unusual, coming in the evening. Don't be too late or I will have gone to bed. I don't want to have to leave the key in the garage.'

I laughed. 'I shouldn't think you'll need to. Expect me mid-evening.'

For a moment, I forgot about the journey with its visit to Gloria and simply enjoyed the thought of being with my aunt in her little cottage with a view of the sea. It was then that I remembered my visit from Freddie and began to wonder why he had told me he was going to Bulgaria when Jim had rung him in Germany. I told myself he probably had meetings in both countries, and to stop trying to see something suspicious in everything.

The next day, Jim arrived a little early. I had made a few sandwiches ready for when he came, thinking that I could take them with me if they weren't wanted. It wouldn't matter if I had double rations. As it was, we had time to eat them and have a coffee before we left. I felt strangely out of sorts – not only because I was doing something that really stretched me, but because I was going off with a man. My mind kept saying, 'What would your mother think?' so I was busy trying to come up with loads of positives to counteract that.

Jim could see I was nervous. He chatted away about how lovely Devon was, even though it was beginning to get colder in London. He talked about the journey, and the views we'd have on the way. I was trying to concentrate, but the minute he finished his sandwiches I cleared them away and quickly washed the cups and plates.

'We're not in a hurry, Jenny, if we can't get the car until two o'clock.'

'I know, but I'd like to get the most difficult bit over with. I can't simply sit here chatting.'

'If the car hire place is closed for lunch, we'll have to wait on the pavement.'

He had a point. 'Okay, I'll check I've got everything I need.'

I fiddled around upstairs. My weekend bag was packed and I knew I didn't need anything. So I made up my face and redid my hair. I was ages in the bathroom. I could hear Jim calling from downstairs. I opened the door.

'Sorry, Jim, were you calling?'

'I wondered if I could pop up and use your bathroom before we go.'

'Yes. Wait a minute and I'll be down.'

I grabbed my weekend bag and handbag from my bedroom and went downstairs.

'I'd have carried that,' said Jim, nodding at the bag.

'No, it's fine. I managed.' I was finding all this very awkward.

While I waited for Jim, I put my coat on. At the last minute I put my wellingtons and anorak ready as well, finding a polythene carrier bag for them. I had no idea whether Gloria's house was out in the country somewhere. Anyway, I would need the wellies if I were to walk near my aunt's house.

'I think we'd better go, Jenny, before you think of something else to take,' said Jim, as he picked up my bag and the carrier.

'I can carry something,' I said. It looked as if Jim had been staying, and I started to think about the neighbours.

'You concentrate on locking up; it's time to go now.'

I didn't need to distract myself as we left the house. I forgot all about the neighbours. Jim started to tell me about going on holiday as a little boy and how he would always take his favourite teddy. That teddy was photographed in loads of different places, although Jim eventually found out that the original one was lost and his mother had come up to London to try to find a copy and rubbed away at its coat to make it look like the missing one.

'She must have been a lovely mum,' I said.

'What was your mum like?'

Tears began to gather in my eyes, but I was able to describe various incidents from my own childhood. The white outfit for a school play that she scorched when she was ironing it dry, so that I was the only ghost in the play with a patch. I hated being on stage and had stayed at the back anyway, even though I had one line which I was meant to say from the front of the stage. I heard the teacher saying to my mother, 'Well, at least she did it. Quite a triumph. You should be proud of her.' She didn't have to tell my mother that: I knew she was proud of me.

It seemed that in no time we had completed the short journey on the Underground and were hurrying towards the exit. I hated going up the escalators to the brightness above and then outside. I shuddered. Jim said nothing but put both the bags in one hand and I felt his hand in mine. I nearly pulled it away, but his smile told me not to. Feeling like a small child, I let him lead me out of the station and along to the car hire firm. I was struggling to breathe and feeling a little dizzy when he stopped and turned to face me. 'Come on, Jenny, you're fine. Breathe a little slower.'

I did. The world stopped spinning and he let go of my hand as we walked into the office to fill in the paperwork.

I had never hired a car with someone else before. I only started to do it when my mother became ill. She used to be the driver in my family because my father's eyesight had never been very good.

'Ah, Mr and Mrs...?'

'No, Miss Jenny Drake. But I asked that my friend's name could go on the contract so that we can share the driving.'

'I see.' The receptionist looked at my overnight bag. There was that look that Trina had given me when I told her Jim was a new friend. Why did I blush when people looked at me like that? It was humiliating. She pushed the forms towards me, together with a battered pen. She turned away.

'I'm not sure about this at all, Jim,' I said, almost whispering.

Jim answered loudly, 'Jenny, your aunt is expecting you to visit and I need to get back to Devon. You don't want to do all the driving – you'll be too tired to enjoy your first evening with her. It's only sensible for us both to drive. If it costs more, I could pay the difference.'

I grinned at him gratefully, feeling a bit better. 'It's not much more, don't worry. It's a long way for me to drive when I'm not used to it.'

The car was a Mini as I had requested. I love Minis – they make me feel very secure and safe down near the road. Jim walked round to the driver's seat and I obediently got into the passenger side. If I started to panic, I would insist on driving. It seems a bit strange, but I would feel safer.

23

Jim was a good driver. He didn't go too fast and seemed aware of what was happening at each junction. After a while I was able to stop mentally co-driving and settle down.

'Have you got a car, Jim?'

'Only a very battered van, which I use to fetch supplies for the café. I need to replace it, really. I didn't dare trust it on a long journey, or I would have fetched you in it.'

'I couldn't have done any of the driving then. I've only driven Minis whenever I've hired a vehicle. I drive so rarely, I wouldn't feel safe in anything else.'

'Do you feel safer in a car than walking?'

'Yes, I suppose I do. It's not quite like being outside. Although I did have a panic attack when I came back from Aunt Judy's last time.'

'What did you do?'

'I calmed myself as much as I could. Come to think of it, I had left the car to go and buy some lunch, and I had a panic attack and struggled to get back in the car. I felt awful, but I managed to slow my breathing and become relaxed enough to start driving again.'

'So that wasn't really while you were in the car?'

'No, I suppose not. I don't remember when I last had a panic attack while I was in the car. Mind you, I was driving.'

'You can drive now, if you like.'

'No, not at the moment. Let's see if I can cope as a passenger.'

'If you're better with a car, I would suggest you buy one. But London is not a good place to be a driver. It took us a good half-hour to get to a clear road.'

'I've worked hard to get as far as the Tube station. I do want to conquer walking around London. And I couldn't imagine living anywhere else.'

'Never? Or for now?'

I looked at Jim. Why was he asking this? I felt the atmosphere charged as it had been before. It felt as if my answer would be massively important. I didn't know what to say. 'I don't know. You can never say "never" about anything, can you?'

Abruptly, Jim changed the subject. 'If we make good time, do you think we ought to go to see Gloria on the way? How ill did she sound when you rang her?'

'Quite bad. But her son has spoken to her since.'

'Yes, he said he was quite worried. Let's try to get there if we can.'

'Okay.'

I tried to work out the timings. It had been two-fifteen when we left the car hire place and it had taken a long time to get out of London. At best we would be in Devon by six-thirty, without a stop, and then we would have to find Gloria's home. We'd be there at least an hour and then would have to drive to Aunt Judy's, via Jim's.

'Jim, I'm not sure we can stop at Gloria's. I told my aunt I'd be there mid-evening. We won't manage it.'

'Let's see how it goes; you can always ring her from Gloria's.' I looked at him, but he was concentrating hard on his driving. We were coming up to a T-junction.

'I'm not sure this is the right way,' he said.

'It is. Take a right here and then it's almost immediately left.'

The next twenty miles or so were taken up with me navigating every turn. Jim seemed to have problems with understanding the instruction, 'Keep on this road!' I have one of those minds that always remembers routes and can even do it going back the other way. We were nearing Wincanton when I became tired of relaying instructions.

'I'll drive now. Pull in somewhere, Jim.'

He looked a bit startled at my tone of voice, but pulled in at the next lay-by. 'Sorry, was I getting on your nerves?'

'Of course not, but it's easier to go for it than keep on telling people the route.'

'How many times have you done this?'

'I've only driven it once, with Aunt Judy that day, but my mother drove me back to see her when I was about thirteen. Usually we went on the train.'

'I knew you were a clever lady, but your geographical awareness is phenomenal.'

'Just a strange skill. Anyway, we're not there yet – there's plenty of time to get thoroughly lost!'

We drove along in silence for a while. It had been raining but now the sun was out. The undulating fields along the side of the A303 looked incredible. We both began to speak at the same time.

'Doesn't it look beautiful?'

'What a lovely day.'

I glanced at Jim as he glanced at me and we both sighed together. We didn't need to say anything. We were good company for each other.

Whenever I drove out in the country, I found myself singing. I tried to stop with Jim there, but a little hum kept coming out every now again as I concentrated on the road. In spite of it being afternoon, I had 'Oh what a beautiful morning' buzzing around my head. One or two notes had been impossible to contain, and then Jim began to sing it out. I laughed and joined in. Two mature adults, in a Mini, singing away as if we were in a music hall. It felt really wonderful.

The special time didn't last long. Doubts crept in, as usual, to spoil the day. Jim probably had no interest in me and was desperate to find out what happened to Henry and why. I was only a useful person to help solve a mystery. And, in my view, far too old to think of anything like romance; that had passed me by. It began to rain again, heavily. My mood began to drop.

We drove on in silence for what seemed like an eternity. I don't know if Jim realised I was sliding downwards, but he began to chatter about nothing much. I was fairly unresponsive.

'Are you all right, Jenny?' he asked.

'I'm concentrating.'

'Let me drive for a bit. I'm pretty sure we'll soon be on familiar ground and I won't need you to guide me.'

'No. I'll be better driving.'

'You don't seem better.'

I wondered whether to talk to him about 'us', if there was an 'us' at all. He had said we would talk about 'us' at some time. Maybe that time hadn't come, or he was dodging it.

'If we find things out at Gloria's, and it solves the mystery, what happens next?'

Jim missed the point. 'I should think we'll have to take the risk then and go to the police.'

'I didn't mean that.'

'What did you mean, then?'

'Never mind, it's not important.'

He didn't press me. We lapsed into silence again. Feeling uncomfortable, I wished I hadn't said anything. I tried to concentrate on thinking about Gloria and how she might be when we got there.

'Jenny, if you're thinking our friendship will end when this is over, I don't want it to.'

'Okay.' I didn't know what else to say, and could feel my face becoming hot. I tried to concentrate on our journey. It seemed to be taking so long. I imagined Gloria being alone in her house, possibly very ill. 'Gloria will still be alive when we get there, won't she?'

'I jolly well hope so. She's made it to what, ninety-two or so? I think she can hang on until we're there.'

'Does she know we're coming?'

'I told Freddie and he said he'd ring her.'

'Did you say we'd be there today or tomorrow?'

'I said we'd try to get there this evening. But if you can't do that, don't worry.'

'What's the time?'

'Four fifty-two.'

'I'll need to stop somewhere for a comfort break soon. Perhaps we should buy takeaways and eat them in the car, taking turns with the driving to save time.'

'Jenny, you're wonderful. Will your aunt be all right about you being later than you said?'

'Probably not. But we can't let down an even older lady, can we?'

It took us fifteen valuable minutes to pull in, use the facilities, refuel and buy something to eat. Jim insisted on me eating my burger and chips before him, so he took over the driving. I hadn't eaten a meal like this for years and I did worry about so much carbohydrate. I ate quickly, concerned that Jim's would be cold, even though I had asked for it to be double wrapped and had then wrapped it in the paper from mine as well. The coffee with it was enough to put me off coffee for life. It bore no resemblance to real coffee at all. I judged Jim's waiting tea would be cold as well as disgusting.

'Okay, I've had enough. Stop where you can and I'll take over.'

I had wiped my hands on my handkerchief but they still smelled of fat and were greasy. I took the sponge for the windscreen, which was slightly damp, and cleaned my hands again, the best I could. I didn't want a slippery steering wheel.

Jim pulled over and we swapped seats. I adjusted the mirror and drove away as he began to attack his semi-cold chips and burger. I wondered again how I had got into all this. I glanced at Jim. That was how. A not terribly good-looking but very kind man from Devon.

'You've got ketchup on your chin,' I told him.

'Oops, thanks, Jen.'

Jen? I savoured it for a moment. No one had called me Jen since my schooldays. I liked it, especially with that soft Devon accent.

24

I was remembering the last time I had come to Devon. Aunt Judy had been in pain with her hip and I spent the whole journey worrying about bumps in the road. She had been cheerful, though, and grateful. In my mind were all the usual fears I had when away from home, but they were dulled because I was with family. There is something very stable about Aunt Judy. I was sorry I would not fulfil her expectations today, because plainly I was going to be late getting to her.

The light was a bit dim; it was such an overcast afternoon. I put the headlights on. I remembered how my father would always say, 'Why have you put the lights on now?' whenever I did that. Maybe with his eyesight failing, he hadn't really recognised that the light was any worse.

At the time, I thought it was an extension of what he would say at home, with the fear always that he wouldn't be able to pay the electricity bill. He was always so frugal that when I took over the accounts after he died, both my mother and I were astounded to find out how well off he had been. We spent money on a painter/decorator immediately, and my mother chose wonderful curtains for all the rooms, bought new beds and had the old sofa recovered. It hardly made a dint in the many thousands of pounds we each had at our disposal. How long ago? More than twenty-five years, and I hadn't decorated since. I realised my house must look very shabby to visitors, namely Jim and Freddie. Oh, and Mike, my psychologist. I promised myself I would refurbish every room when I was back home, and order some new outfits while I was at it. It was time I spent some of my inheritance.

I glanced sideways at Jim. He seemed to be asleep. I remembered that he had been up early to catch the train and had been travelling virtually all day. No wonder he hadn't wanted me to hurry him over lunch. I felt guilty that I had cleared things away so quickly.

Jim slept while we went up to the motorway and then dropped down it to turn off. We were halfway up the A361 when he woke.

'Where are we? Have I been asleep?'

'Yes, you were sleeping. You obviously needed it. We're on the A361 heading towards Barnstaple.'

'Nearly there, then. I have some directions for getting to Gloria's house here somewhere.'

He leant over to the back seat and rummaged around in his coat pocket. He found what he wanted. A tightly folded, used envelope. He spread it out and held it in several positions. It was too dark to read it so we had to pull over. Even with the interior light on, he couldn't decipher it.

'I shouldn't have written the directions in pencil,' said Jim.

'Let me see.'

The scribbled words were very idiosyncratic notes. I could make out 'trn rt' and there were a couple of circles which must be roundabouts. Some of the writing was too faint to see at all.

'Did we bring a torch?' he said, as if we had packed together.

'As a matter of fact, I did. But it's in my bag in the boot.'

Jim got out and fetched my weekend bag. I rifled through it, untidying my clothes. I was conscious of him watching me. I didn't want him to see into the bag: it felt too intrusive.

'Here it is.' I passed it to Jim and zipped up the bag.

'Ah, here we go. The directions start from Exeter when we take the A38. Do you know it?'

I said nothing, but sat there wondering how to tell him we had a problem.

'What's the matter?' asked Jim.

'Bad news, Jim. We should have come the other way if we're going via Exeter. What's her actual address?'

'What do you mean, the other way?'

'It's the other side of Devon, near the east side of Dartmoor. Pass me the map; there'll be one in the glove compartment.'

Jim fished about in the compartment. 'There isn't one.'

'There must be, there always is.'

'There isn't one, Jenny!'

'What's the name of the village or town where Gloria lives?'

'Well, the postcode is EX something. Let's see. The village is near to Bridford.'

'I thought we were heading for Bideford!'

'No, it's definitely Bridford, Jenny. I have it written here.'

What had happened to 'Jen'? I realised I had been speaking sharply.

'I'm sorry, Jim. It's only that I'm not sure what to do now.'

'Let's stop at the next garage and see if they sell maps – perhaps we can cut back.'

We drove along in silence. Garages seemed to have disappeared. I couldn't actually remember where they were along this road; I obviously had no need of them when I had come before. Eventually we found one. Jim went in, but came out shaking his head.

'They didn't have one. But I've been given the route to Bridford – I made sure they knew it was the village near Exeter.'

I looked at his scribbled directions. It looked as if Bridford was on the edge of Dartmoor. It would take maybe an hour to get there, then there was the journey back to Jasmine Cottage – not too far from Bideford – to think about. I glanced at my watch. Even if we were to find a short cut, it would probably be an hour before we would arrive at Gloria's.

'It's nearly seven already. Should we postpone our visit to Gloria until tomorrow?'

'I don't think so; we may regret it.'

He was right. I thought of my aunt waiting at Jasmine Cottage, but there wasn't much I could do. I turned the car and we set off. Jim was reading out the instructions he had been given by the garage. I felt uncomfortable relying on him to guide me. But after twenty minutes, I realised that the instructions were taking us back the way we came and dropping us down the motorway to Exeter.

'We're retracing our steps. It will take a long time, but at least I will know the roads for most of it.'

Jim grunted in reply. I wondered if I'd sounded sharp again. I was feeling irritated by him. I could have saved an hour at least by going direct to Bridford.

'Let's put our heads together and see if we can work out how your instructions fit with this route, Jim. Have you any road numbers on there?'

Jim put on the torch again, as I switched on the interior light. Together, using both sets of instructions, we worked out the point at which we would have to use the instructions again.

Thirty minutes later we were nearing the pub in Gloria's village. The road had been dark and difficult to drive along in the rain. A red car that had been right behind us stopped, but didn't draw into the pub car park.

'Jim, has that car been following us for long?' I asked.

'What car?'

I pointed it out. Jim shook his head. 'I haven't noticed. Probably not. No one knows we're here.'

I felt too exhausted to think about it. Jim went into the pub to get directions. I wanted to go in and ring Aunt Judy, but the urge to simply hide away and stay in the safety of the car was far greater.

'Move over,' he said as he got in.

'Surely we're nearly there,' I said. 'I could drive the last bit.'

'No, you're tired. I'll take you.'

Jim turned the car round and drove back up the hill. The car I had noticed appeared to start up but I didn't see whether it followed us round the bend of the road. After about two hundred yards, Jim turned left up a farm track. There in front of us was a huge farmhouse. Only one light was on in a room at the front.

'Here is Gloria's house!' he said triumphantly.

'You tease – we could have walked up here from where we were parked!'

It was only a few slightly muddy steps to Gloria's front door. Jim took my arm as I got out of the car. The world seemed vast and unfriendly. I felt my breathing go into overdrive. I froze.

'Come on,' he said. 'Gloria needs you.'

I calmed myself and rang her bell. A dog barked, then silence. I pressed it again.

'I think we should go in if the door's open,' said Jim. 'She hasn't been seen in the village for a week. People were thinking she's away.'

'We know she's not away: she spoke to me from her house phone.'

We tried once again with the doorbell. Again the dog barked, then nothing. Jim tried the handle. I was trembling all over as we stepped into the house, my shoes clattering on the flagstones.

'You'll have to go first,' said Jim. 'I might scare her.'

I pushed on the door which had the light coming from under it. 'Gloria,' I called. 'It's Jenny Drake, come to visit.'

A black and white collie came bounding towards me. I'm not at my best with strange dogs, but I knew to stand and let him sniff at me. He did so, then whined. I followed the dog into the room. He went round to the front of the armchair by the ashes of a fire and put his head on his mistress' lap. I moved round to say 'hello' again. The very old lady with folds of wrinkled pale skin did not move. I thought she was dead.

'Jim, come quickly.'

I lifted her cold arm and felt for her pulse. Nothing. I pulled away her shawl and tried the pulse in her neck; her neck was warmer. My fingers probed gently, then more firmly. 'She has a pulse, Jim.'

Jim had gone. I could hear him talking in the hall and realised he was ringing for an ambulance. I grabbed throws from the sofa and wrapped them around her, all the time saying, 'Gloria, can you hear me? It's Jenny here. Gloria, can you hear me?'

There was the merest of sighs. I couldn't remember my first aid – so many years since I had been in the Girl Guides. I unwrapped the throws and put my head against her chest. Yes, I could hear a faint heartbeat. What should I do?

Jim came in. 'The ambulance is on its way.'

'Should we put her in the recovery position, Jim? I can't remember my first aid.'

'Keep talking to her, I think, and make sure she's warm but can breathe.'

'It's cold in here.'

'I'll see if I can find a heater. And I'll see if I can make you a cup of tea. You look awful.'

I realised I was shivering. 'Not yet. I think we'd better try to lie her down first. Perhaps on the sofa.'

'I can lift her over there; she looks as if she hardly weighs anything.'

The dog moved back from her as if he understood. I stroked Gloria's hand. 'Gloria, you need to lie down. We're going to put you on the sofa. Jim will lift you.'

Jim lifted Gloria up as if she were nothing. He gently lowered her onto the sofa. There seemed to be a flicker of her eyelids as he laid her among the soft cushions. Together we turned her on to her side, propping her with cushions. I covered her with the throws again.

'Perhaps you can fetch me a cardigan from my bag. The big grey one.' It didn't matter any more if he went to my bag. Gloria needed me to stay here.

'Gloria, if you can hear me, squeeze my hand.' Nothing. I squeezed hers gently, then tried again. 'Gloria, please squeeze my hand.' Her hand lay limp on mine. I waited, wondering what to do, then there was the slightest movement.

'Well done, Gloria, well done. I'm Jenny. We spoke on the phone. I need to know if you can hear me, so please squeeze my hand every now and again. You seem to be quite ill, so we're getting you some help.'

I couldn't think of anything else to say, so I repeated it all again.

Jim brought the right cardigan from my bag. This was for me, not Gloria. I was so cold that her hand now felt warm in mine. Jim helped me put the cardigan on while I changed hands as I put each of my arms into the sleeves.

'I'll go on the heater hunt,' said Jim, 'then I'll ring Freddie. He needs to know what's going on.'

I nodded, then turned my attention back to Gloria, making sure that all of her was covered up by the throws. I started talking to her again.

'Are you feeling any warmer, Gloria? It won't be long now until we have some help. Another squeeze of my hand would be useful.'

The slight change in her hand position was less than the previous squeeze. I was scared she might die before the ambulance arrived. Inside I was praying, 'Dear God, help her make it.' But I knew that at her age it was highly likely that her time was up.

Jim had found a fan heater and set it going. I checked Gloria's forehead. Still cool. I didn't want to overheat her if she had a temperature already. I realised I had been kneeling on the rug for rather longer than my legs liked. I let go of Gloria's hand and tried to stand up. I had dreadful pins and needles in my feet.

I clutched at Jim as he helped me reach the armchair. The pain in my feet was excruciating, but I didn't want to stay too far away. I propped myself on the arm of the sofa and found myself praying a real prayer, with a fervency I scarcely remembered ever having before.

I looked up. Jim too had his eyes closed, his lips gently moving. I waited until he opened them. 'Can you move that other chair over here, by Gloria? I need to sit by her.'

Back by her side, with my feet still smarting, I stroked Gloria's hand and resumed talking to her. We offered her a drink of water, but with no response; I thought we'd better not try to give it to her.

Eventually, we heard the ambulance coming up the track. Jim and I had to stand back and wait while the medics attended to her. They shot questions at us, which we didn't know the answers to. All we knew was her age, address and that she had one son. In the end I found her handbag, and feeling very invasive I pulled out a small address book and her pension book. At least I had her date of birth, which I gave to the paramedics. I remembered to tell them she had thought she might have bronchitis and had been coughing continuously when I last spoke to her on the phone.

They took her pulse, checked her breathing and temperature and gave her some oxygen before finally moving her onto a stretcher, ready to take her to hospital.

'Would you come in the ambulance with her?' The question was directed at me. I looked horrified at Jim, who mouthed 'You can do it.' Swallowing hard, I followed the stretcher out to the ambulance and climbed in.

In the bright lights inside the ambulance, Gloria looked as if she had already gone. Her face was grey and she seemed to have stopped breathing, but the ambulance man seemed unconcerned. He hooked her up to a drip, though.

'You'd best speak to her,' he told me. 'She may respond to you.'

I talked to her again, encouraging her to squeeze my hand. No movement.

'Do you think she can hear me?'

'Most probably. Keep talking – we all need to hear the sound of a familiar voice.'

I didn't like to start explaining the shortness of our acquaintance. I spoke soothingly as before. It was more difficult with the paramedics listening.

I felt like a spare part once we arrived at the hospital. I followed them in, then leant against a wall while various doctors came and examined her. 'Come this way, we're taking her through to the cubicle.'

Obediently, I followed. The bile was rising in my throat, I felt so nervous. This time it was not only my anxiety that was causing me to panic, but also the genuine fear of what would happen to Gloria. I had quite forgotten the reason why we had come in the first place. I realised I had failed to phone my aunt. I started to look into my handbag for my purse to find some money for a phone, when I found that the bag I had in my hand was Gloria's.

I was left with Gloria for more than an hour and could do nothing. She was checked every ten minutes or so by one or other of the nurses. I watched the drip as it left its head-high polythene container and imagined the flow of it into her arm. She was receiving oxygen through a mask and was linked to a monitor which bleeped rhythmically. I held her hand every now and again and talked to her a little. Only once she squeezed my hand, but her colour was coming back. Now she looked as if she were sleeping, not already dead.

Jim put his head round the curtain. 'I've had to lie to get in,' he whispered. 'I'm afraid I'm Gloria's nephew. How have you got in?'

'I don't know,' I said softly. 'I think I came as part of the package.'

'I brought your handbag in case you need it,' he said, in a normal voice.

'Thank goodness. Do you know where there's a phone? Aunt Judy will be desperate by now. It's nearly ten o'clock.'

I told Gloria I would be back in a few minutes and that Jim was here in case she needed him. I've no idea whether or not she heard me. A nurse directed me to the payphone.

'Aunt Judy, I'm all right but we called in to see a friend on the way to you and she is very ill. I'm at the hospital now.'

I think my aunt had been asleep because she asked who I was several times, then suddenly became herself. 'What do you mean, "we", and who is this friend?'

'It's a long story, Aunt Judy. I'll tell you in the morning. Please leave the key out so I can get in.'

'The key's out already, I couldn't wait up any longer. Really, Jenny, this is quite unlike you. It is very inconsiderate.'

'My friend is very ill, I had to get her to hospital.' I was careful not to say 'we' again.

'Well, be as quick as you can.'

'I will be. Thank you, Aunt Judy, and I'll see you in the morning.'

I walked back to the cubicle. The doctor there was talking to Jim about his 'aunt'. I was so tired I couldn't concentrate on what was being said. I slumped into the chair and waited.

'We can go,' said Jim. 'They're going to sedate her tonight, rehydrate her, give her some antibiotics and then see how she is in the morning. The doctor said to be prepared for the worst.'

It was quite a tearful farewell to Gloria. I suppose that was because the last few hours had been so emotional. I gave her a hug and touched her hand. She turned hers over and briefly our palms met.

'Keep going, Gloria. You can do it. I'll be back tomorrow.'

25

Jim drove us to my aunt's cottage. It was just as well because I could hardly keep my eyes open. He seemed to have a rough idea where to go but shook me awake a couple of miles away. I surfaced enough to direct him and to put my shoes back on. I couldn't recall removing them.

We arrived at Jasmine Cottage.

'Where does she leave the key?' asked Jim.

I sent him to find it on the hook in the garage, and, as quietly as I could, I took my bag from the back seat. I was waiting on the doorstep when Jim brought the key.

'Is this the one?' he whispered.

'Should be.'

He passed me the car keys.

'No, you'll have to take the car,' I said, 'or you can't get back.'

'I could call a cab.'

'No, the phone is in the hall, you'll wake Aunt Judy. You take the car. I'll explain you gave me a lift.'

'Okay.'

I unlocked the door and turned round to say goodbye.

Jim took the bag from me and placed it on the step, then gave me a big hug. I leant against him briefly, too tired to work out what the hug might mean, or even think about it.

I gave him a quick peck on the cheek. 'Goodnight, Jim. See you tomorrow. Give me time to sleep in a bit.'

'Goodnight, Jen. Sleep well, dear.'

I stepped into the cottage and closed the door behind me. Then, taking my weekend bag, I went upstairs and quietly let myself into the spare bedroom. I was startled by a loud shout: 'Jenny! Come here.'

Obediently, I walked into my aunt's bedroom. She was sitting upright, propped by her pillows, her long grey hair spread loose around her. Her eyes were startlingly bright.

'What's this all about, Jenny? Why were you whispering to some man who's driven off? Were you really at the hospital?'

'Can I tell you in the morning, Aunt Judy?'

'No, I need to know now. I've been really worried about you, then somebody simply drops you off. Where's your car?'

'I don't have one, Aunt Judy. I hire one when I need it. Don't you remember I went to hire a car when I brought you back?'

'So who was the man who drove you here?'

'That's Jim. I met him last time I was here. He lives in Devon and was coming back from London too.'

'So where have you been all evening?'

'In the hospital.'

I explained that it was a lady I had wanted to visit, and that we'd called in on the way and found her to be very ill.

'Well, you might have rung me earlier than you did; I didn't know where you were.'

'I left my handbag in Gloria's house when I went in the ambulance, so I didn't have any money to ring you. Not

163

until Jim brought it to me, then I rang you as soon as I could.'

'Well, we had better talk about it all in the morning. I've waited up long enough for you now. What's the time?'

'Gone midnight. I'm exhausted. Goodnight, Aunt Judy, and I'm really sorry you were worried.'

My aunt sighed. She stopped looking at me and pushed one pillow from behind her onto the floor, to lie back against the others. I leaned forward and popped a kiss on her forehead. She closed her eyes and muttered, 'Goodnight.'

Slightly ashamed that I had told her some half-truths, I went back and quickly got myself to bed. I lay there for a while, praying for my aunt and for Gloria. My troubled conscience steadied a little and didn't stop me falling into a deep sleep.

The grilling I had received in the night continued over breakfast. Aunt Judy's questions came thick and fast. I felt irritated. I was a grown woman who had acted in the best way I knew, and I was being treated like an errant schoolgirl.

'Aunt Judy, it is really kind of you to put me up at such short notice. I'm sorry I didn't make it clear to you that I would not be alone on the journey. I have my reasons for needing someone with me.'

My aunt looked crestfallen. I realised I had spoken sharply to her. 'I'm sorry. I think I'd better explain.'

So I did. I told her about the agoraphobia, how I had tried to sort myself out by going to the beach, the panic that then overwhelmed me, the way Jim had calmed me and the fact that he knew about the man who had jumped. Aunt Judy interrupted me. 'I was there, Jenny. We thought you were pretending, and then we found out that the man had committed suicide. Did you see him jump?'

'Yes. I did.' For the first time since it happened, I did not feel the fear when I talked about it. My aunt sat there quietly, thinking. 'So, was it Gloria Standish that you went to see?'

'Yes! Do you know her?'

'Of course I do. She used to be a very important person. Still is, I suppose. People knew her for miles around. She was always organising charity events. She did badges for the Brownies and the Guides, I can't remember what exactly.'

It occurred to me that it would be really ironic if she were the one who had taught me first aid. I couldn't remember her from Brownies or Guides, though.

'She was in a really bad way. It's a good job we called in last night rather than leave it until today.'

Never one to mince her words, Aunt Judy asked, 'Do you think she'll die?'

'I don't know, Aunt Judy. I'll ring the hospital if you don't mind and see how she is.'

'No, of course I don't. You go ahead while I clear up the dishes.'

I found the number and rang from the hall. It took a while to be put through to the right ward. As soon as I said who I was, the nurse asked if I was the Jenny who had come in with Mrs Standish.

'Yes, that's me.'

'Why didn't you tell us you were her adopted daughter? She's been asking for you over and over again. Come in as soon as you can.'

I was caught off guard. I nearly denied being any relative, adopted or otherwise, but wasn't sure I should. I focused on why I had rung. 'So she's much better, is she?'

'Fighting fit, I'd say! No, that's an exaggeration, but she's certainly able to say what she wants today. Your mother's a strong lady.'

I laughed, mostly with relief. 'Thank you for all you're doing. Please tell her I hope to come in later this morning, but I'll have to arrange a lift.'

'She'll be very pleased. And she wants you to bring in a box file from the loft. She says you'll know which one.'

'I'll see if I can do that.'

I put the phone on the receiver and wondered what I'd done. Here I was, going along with Gloria's lie, when perhaps I should have explained. Now Jim and I would have to go to get the box file. I hoped Jim hadn't posted the key through the door, if he'd locked up when leaving the house. At least I could find Gloria an overnight bag and a few personal belongings to have in hospital too. I was about to ring Jim, but then I put the phone back on the cradle.

I went to explain gently to Aunt Judy that I needed to go back to the hospital.

'If you must,' she said. 'But I don't really see what it's got to do with you.' I didn't want to tell her that we were all working to uncover the truth about Henry's death.

'We talked on the phone. I think she sees me as a friend. And it was me who found her and Jim who called the ambulance. I don't think she has anyone else around when her son is away.'

'Well, don't let her take advantage, will you?'

'No, I won't.'

Jim came to pick me up within half an hour. By then I had satisfied Aunt Judy's curiosity a little more by explaining that I had hired the car and we were both named as drivers so that we could share the driving, and that he had needed it to get back home the previous night.

'I'll drop him off at some point so that we can have the car. Maybe we can go for a little jaunt.'

'That would be nice dear, if you have the time. When will you be back?'

'I'm not sure. We're picking up a few things for Gloria first.'

'You can bring your friend back if you want to, dear.'

'Thank you, but I'm not sure that would be appropriate.'

So when Jim came and knocked at the door, I was really hoping he wouldn't put his arm round me. He didn't, but did ask to say 'hello' to Aunt Judy.

So I took him into the living room and introduced him to her. They shook hands rather formally, then Jim said, 'I am so sorry to have disturbed you last night. If there had been any way of getting Jenny here quicker, I would have done so. Events somehow took over.'

'Well, I hope Mrs Standish gets better after all this excitement.'

Jim looked a little startled. I quickly explained. 'My aunt remembers Mrs Standish. She was quite an important member of the community in her younger days.' Before he could say anything, I added, 'But we must go. Aunt Judy and I have plans for this afternoon so I need to get back as soon as possible.'

Jim said goodbye and we went out to the car. 'Why did you tell her it was Gloria Standish?' he asked.

'I told her how I met you and she just realised which Gloria it must be. I think I could tell her everything, in fact, although it might frighten her a little.'

'Would she be inclined to gossip?'

'Not Aunt Judy; she'd never tell a soul if we asked her not to.'

We turned up the track towards Gloria's house. There was a battered Ford Escort in the drive.

'We may need your cover story, Jenny, to say why we were here yesterday.'

'Ah yes – I'm a writer! No problem, my notebook's in my bag. But getting to the door is a bigger challenge.'

Jim got out first and walked round to the passenger door to open it for me. I clung to him as we walked to the front door. We realised it was open. As soon as we stepped into the hall, he sat me on the nearest chair. I was shaking.

'I'll find out who's here.'

'I think it's a cleaner,' I said, between shudders.

'How do you know?'

'Sound of a Hoover.'

Jim went to the bottom of the stairs and called up. Nothing happened.

'She won't hear you if she's vacuuming,' I said. 'Wait till the noise stops.' I felt a bit more together now, and really pleased with myself that I'd been able to think while I was struggling not to panic. Another milestone for me.

We waited in the hall for a few minutes, and sure enough, the hum whined as it slowed down and stopped. Jim called up, and a middle-aged lady leant over the banisters.

'Yes, what do you want?'

Jim explained that we were 'friends' of Gloria and that we'd found her the previous evening. The cleaner came down the stairs, the duster over the banister as she moved. Gloria's dog came down with her, going straight to Jim for a stroke.

'So she's in hospital, is she? They said she might be, in the shop this morning. I'll take Charlie back with me.' The dog turned when she said 'Charlie' and moved towards her as if he understood.

'That's kind of you, to take the dog,' said Jim.

'He'll be all right with me, won't you, boy?' The dog wagged his tail enthusiastically. She continued, 'What ward's she on? I might send a card.' She stopped, and put a hand up to her mouth. 'She ain't dead, is she?'

We reassured her and told her we were collecting a few things she wanted. I couldn't think how we were going to get into the loft without her knowing. We didn't even know where the access to the loft was.

'I'm going to need your help,' I said. 'I have no idea what nighties she wears or what else I should take. In fact, I don't even know where her bedroom is.'

'Come with me,' she said. 'I'll show you.'

Gloria had a room with an en suite bathroom, which was near the end of the corridor upstairs. I followed the cleaner into the room, and she told me her name – Mary Davies – as we went. Together we found some nightwear for Gloria as well as some day clothes in case she was allowed out of bed. Mary Davies disappeared into the bathroom to find facial wipes, flannel, toothbrush and other toiletries that may be of use. Together we hunted for her spongebag, and eventually discovered it at the back of her nightie drawer. We collected quite a pile of items and I spotted a huge carrier bag at the back of her wardrobe to put them in. I kept thinking of other things and took as long as I possibly could over it all, hoping that Jim would have a chance to find the box file. When we came out of the bedroom I was horrified to see Jim's legs at the top of the loft ladder.

'I've found her little suitcase,' he called. 'She told me it would be up here.'

I gave the bag of clothes to the cleaner and took the suitcase from Jim. From its weight I knew he'd found the box file. I also knew Gloria wouldn't have been able to tell Jim to fetch a suitcase from there. It occurred to me that he was quite good at lying.

'Let me give it a quick dust,' said the cleaner.

'Don't worry. If you pass me a duster, I'll do it,' I said. 'And would it be possible to make up a bed for Gloria downstairs, in case she's too weak to get up here when she comes out of hospital? Her big settee might do.'

'She has a day bed in the other room. I could make that up.'

'Even better. I'll get this lot downstairs and sort it out, then we'll be off.'

Luckily she didn't follow us, so she didn't see me quickly tip the contents of the carrier into the suitcase on top of the box file, before we left.

'She was very trusting,' I said, as we got in the car.

'Well, we rescued Gloria. I suppose that gave us some sort of credibility.'

'But we might not have been who we said we were.'

'Perhaps someone described me to her – the pub was pretty full when I went in to ask for directions.'

We reached the hospital quickly. Jim dropped me off fairly close to the hospital doors, but the minute he drove off to park, I became breathless and panicky. I leant against a pillar, looking at the building, as I gained control over my breathing. I managed to walk alongside a row of ambulances and into the foyer. I sat on the nearest chair, waiting for Jim. He was carrying the small suitcase.

We went straight up to the ward. I was glad he hadn't seen me struggling to get into the hospital.

'I'm Jenny,' I said to one of the nurses I hadn't seen before. 'I've come to visit Gloria Standish.'

'Last bed on the left. She's been desperate to see you.' She turned to Jim. 'I wonder if you'd mind waiting over there? Some of the ladies become a little worried when there are male visitors out of visiting hours.'

Jim raised his eyebrows at me but obediently took a seat round the corner to the main ward. I found Gloria, lying on her back, with her head supported by a single pillow. I looked at her for a few minutes, simply marvelling at how different her face looked. So much better. She opened her eyes and struggled a little as she pulled herself up.

171

'Arrange my pillows, Jenny, like any good daughter – there's one on the chair.'

I grinned at her and did as I was told. I decided I would have quite enjoyed being this lady's daughter. She had style, even now, sat up in bed in an awful NHS nightdress that was all open at the back. She looked around her at the other patients as if surveying a room full of students. I remembered what Aunt Judy said about her always organising things.

'I have a suitcase full of your stuff,' I told her, 'including some nighties and underwear, a couple of books and toiletries.'

'I knew you'd make an excellent daughter when I decided to adopt you,' she said, 'but did you find that other thing? You must have been in the loft to fetch the suitcase.'

'Yes, Jim went up in the loft and brought down both the case and the other thing. Do you want it here?'

'No, that's fine. You and Jim look after it for now.'

We smiled a conspiratorial smile and I went into dutiful visiting daughter mode. I couldn't quite call her 'Mum', though; that term had belonged to my own mother.

'How have you been? Do you know how long you'll be in here?'

'I think the doctor wants to talk to you.' She stopped speaking to cough. Her lungs sounded wheezy as the cough subsided.

I was being drawn in too deeply, because of her pretence. 'But I don't know enough about you if he asks.'

'I thought of that, dear. That's the trouble with late adoptions.' I couldn't help smiling; she was a very clever lady. She carried on, 'I know how forgetful you are so I've noted a few things to jog your memory.' She inclined her head to one side and I turned to look. I realised that the lady in the next bed was leaning slightly towards us although she was looking at the opposite wall. Gloria handed me a list scribbled on an old envelope that she had presumably had in her handbag. I read it through, wondering how much I would remember if I were to talk to a doctor.

'So he hasn't told you what's wrong?' I asked

'Well, early stages of hypothermia, so it's a good job you got there before the old ticker gave out. But he wants to talk to you about this cough. I had an X-ray this morning, but as I'm of such great age he seems to think I shouldn't know the results. What he'd do with them if my adoptive daughter wasn't here, I don't know.'

'He would probably ring Freddie.'

'I didn't bring his phone number. Anyway, he's abroad.'

'Jim had the number; he rang him and will ring again when we leave here.'

'Well, that's extraordinarily kind of him.'

'Well, he is your nephew!' There was a moment's pause as Gloria assimilated the fact that she now had two new relatives. I didn't go on to explain that Jim had talked his way on to the ward by saying he was related.

'I suppose he is. I'd forgotten that, silly old me. Perhaps he should talk to the doctor too. I'll make sure the nurse knows I want the doctor to speak to you both.'

'We'll tell Freddie we're holding the fort for now, shall we? He's on standby to hurry back from his trip.'

'See what the doctor says first and then tell him. If I've only a day or two before I pop my clogs, I don't want to leave him out of the show!'

I laughed. 'I don't think there's any chance of that: you have way too much to do. You can't leave us now!'

'Good point, dear, good point.'

The nurse interrupted us. 'The doctor would like to talk to you, Miss Drake, before he does his rounds.'

Gloria spoke up, 'My nephew's here. He'd best go in to the powwow too. I want them both there.'

I left Gloria, squeezing her hand. 'I'll be back soon,' I said.

The nurse collected Jim and we both went into a small office. Dr Crisp looked like his name – very neat and tidy. We were introduced to him as 'Miss Drake, adopted daughter, and Mr Tyler, nephew'. I perched on a slightly grubby navy chair and tried to calm my nerves.

The doctor spoke quickly and quite dispassionately, I thought. 'Your mother has had a persistent cough for more than a month. Her health has deteriorated sharply. She probably hasn't eaten. She self-medicated and reached the point where she was too weak to move and probably fell asleep in her chair. She was in a coma when the paramedics picked her up.'

He looked over his glasses at us as if we were the cause of all her problems.

'We spoke to her on the phone,' explained Jim, 'and she played down her symptoms. We drove up from London and called in on her because we were worried.'

'Just as well you did. She was very poorly, but has already begun to recover.'

We both nodded. The doctor's tone softened. 'We X-rayed her this morning and we didn't like what we saw. Do you know if Mrs Standish has been coughing up blood?'

'No, she didn't tell me,' I said.

Jim added, 'Nor me.'

'Probably she has been for some time. She has a shadow on her left lung which looks rather sinister.'

'It's not cancer, is it?' I may have become her adoptive daughter very recently, but I was as fearful for Gloria as if she were really my mother.

'I'm afraid that is what we suspect.'

'She looks so much better,' I said.

The doctor watched as I took my handkerchief out of my bag. I didn't have to pretend; I couldn't hold back the tears.

Jim was left to talk to the doctor while I recovered myself. 'Do you know how long she'll have?' he asked.

'It depends how advanced it is. Maybe a week or two, or a few months.'

'I think I had better call her son,' said Jim. 'He'll want to come back from Germany.'

I nodded and stood up. 'Should we talk to her about it?'

'Prepare her – let her know we are investigating further. She may have some affairs to put in order.'

As we walked out of the room, Jim's arm around my shoulder steadied me.

The nurse was pulling the curtains around Gloria's bed as I walked back down the ward. She turned and said, 'Fetch your cousin; he can talk to your mother, too.' For a moment I couldn't think who she meant, but then I went and found Jim. Together we went into the shrouded area surrounding Gloria.

'Oh dear,' she said as we sat either side of her. 'Long faces. I suppose I've got cancer?'

'You may have,' I said. 'There is a suspicious shadow on your lungs.'

'Oh, sugar!' she shouted. It startled us both, but before we could say anything, she added, almost in a whisper, 'I wanted to sort this mystery bit out once and for all, and now this. You two had better get on with finding stuff out quickly.'

Jim and I looked at each other, astounded. Then we both spoke to Gloria together.

'Yes, Aunt Gloria.'

'Yes, Mother.'

'Get on with it, then. Off you go.'

I tidied her pillow and straightened her bedding over her.

Gloria lay back. As I put away the toiletries and towels and folded the clothes into the bottom of her bedside cabinet, she turned and watched me. 'Has anyone fed my dog?' she asked.

I was able to reassure her that Mary Davies would take care of Charlie. I was giving her a hug as Jim pulled back the curtains. We passed the doctor on his rounds. Jim paused to tell him, 'She's taken it well, I think. But she asked us to go.'

The doctor nodded briefly and turned back to speak to the Sister about another patient.

'All in a day's work for him,' said Jim. 'Let's have a cup of tea before you drive me home to read stuff and you go to look after your real elderly relative.'

'Good plan. I'm ready for some normality.'

'Whatever that is,' said Jim.

26

When I got back, Aunt Judy immediately put her coat on. 'I've worked out our little jaunt,' she said. 'There's a lovely café on the way to the garden centre, where we can have lunch, and then we can go to Barnstaple and look at antique shops and maybe have tea in The Best Teapot. What do you think?'

The thought horrified me. I didn't know if I would get into all these places, or how far we would have to walk out in the open in Barnstaple. Garden centres were not too bad once I was indoors, but I would have trouble walking out among the plants. 'I do have a bit of a problem with being outside, so we will need places we can drive to.'

'You're not that bad, are you?'

I sat on one of the pine chairs round the kitchen table. She pulled out a chair opposite. I looked straight into her eyes as I began to explain. 'I panic when I'm out in the open. It has taken me more than six months to be able to walk from my home to the Tube station – do you remember where that is? It's not quite so hard when someone is with me, but I still find it really difficult.'

My aunt looked steadily at me. 'It's that bad?'

'Yes. Sometimes worse, sometimes better. I can manage the garden centre if it's not too far from where we have to park. Is there parking right near the café on the way there?'

'No, not really. It's behind the café and you have to walk round. But there is a pub nearby. If it's not too busy we could park right near the entrance there.'

'That would be better for me.'

'We could pick up your friend afterwards, and he could drive and drop us right outside the big antique shop and then take us to The Best Teapot.'

It was beginning to sound more manageable. I rang Jim and arranged to collect him at about three-thirty. My aunt was putting on her scarf and pulled on some red leather gloves which matched her red leather shoes; both looked new. It occurred to me that she might not get out that often. I wished I lived nearer.

All went reasonably to plan. Aunt Judy suggested emphatically that I park in the disabled area in the garden centre. In the end I did, because everywhere else was too far to walk.

'I'll tell them you have problems if they make a fuss,' she said. That didn't really help me feel good about it. She only wanted indoor plants, to brighten the house up, but bought me a big pot of pansies to go outside my front door. I didn't like to tell her what a state my garden was in, but accepted it gracefully. Carrying things to the car was difficult for me – not because of the weight but because of the sheer enormity of outside.

'I'm sorry, dear, you had to go back for all those pots of flowers.' I looked at Aunt Judy. I wasn't sure she was sorry at all.

By the time we reached the pub it was pouring with rain. There was a space quite near the door and we both made a dash for it under Aunt Judy's massive golfing umbrella. That was easier; I was indoors before I could hardly think about it.

While we waited for our order to come, Aunt Judy was chatting away about old times and old friends. I was trying to keep up with all the names when one stood out – 'Gloria'.

'Is that Gloria Standish?'

'Yes, but she was plain old "Brown" then. She lived in the next village to me and was much older. Good ten years, maybe more. She was in the Guides before I went to Brownies. She sometimes came to our church, though.'

'Which church was that?'

Aunt Judy gave me a stare and sat up very straight, '*The* church, dear, Anglican.'

'Oh, sorry. We were Quakers.'

'I know, dear.' She looked at me as if I were to be pitied.

I moved away from that part of the conversation. 'But getting back to Gloria, did you know her when she met Henry?'

'Her husband? She met him when she went to university. York, I think she went. Somewhere miles from Devon, anyway. I can remember the wedding, although I wasn't a guest. There was a children's choir and we sang something. I don't think it went very well.'

'Did she work here after she was married?'

'Yes, in the school. She worked there for years. But she had a son and stopped for a while. Henry was a policeman.

Could never understand that; he went to university and then he was a policeman.'

'You have to have brains to be a policeman.'

'But catching robbers and pickpockets isn't a gentleman's trade. He came from a really good family.'

I decided not to argue. Aunt Judy had some odd ideas sometimes, but then it was a different era and I wasn't an authority on what people thought about professions then.

'Did they both have a good reputation?'

'Oh yes, despite Henry being a Roman Catholic. That was really strange; she carried on being Anglican when he was Catholic.'

'Was it a good marriage?'

'I don't know, dear. You'll have to ask her when she's well enough.'

I nearly told Aunt Judy that she was well enough to have lied about who I was, but I thought I had better not.

The food arrived and we both became quiet as we ate a delicious roast dinner. Mine was lamb, and Aunt Judy had chosen chicken. We didn't talk about Gloria or Henry again, but our conversation focused on places to eat and which pubs did good roasts and how expensive they were. I enjoyed thinking about ordinary things.

By the time Aunt Judy had eaten a dessert and I'd finished my coffee, it was gone three o'clock. We hurried out of the pub.

'I won't be ready for a cream tea at four,' I told Aunt Judy.

'Nor I, dear. But we have to collect your friend now or he will worry where you have got to.'

So we drove towards the coast to collect Jim. The weather was still cloudy and it had begun to get cold. Jim was ready, and I moved into the back of the car so that he could drive.

'Next stop The Best Teapot?' he asked.

'No, we still have time to go to the Antiques Centre. If you drop us right outside, then you can come in to join us, if you like.'

It only took ten minutes. I put up the brolly as we left the car and crossed the road into the centre. It was cold in there and smelled damp and musty. I was reminded a little of Gloria's house. Aunt Judy was mostly interested in the china. Together we peered into cabinets and looked closely at items on the shelves, exclaiming at their delicacy or exquisite design. I couldn't imagine how she would fit anything else into her already overflowing china cabinet, but I did think the four small jugs she wanted to buy were delightful.

Jim joined us at about cabinet two of the dozen or so we looked at. Each time Aunt Judy moved a little ahead, he told me about a document from the box file.

'There's a ration book belonging to the first man who jumped, and notes about a visit to his wife.' I longed to ask him what the notes said and what Dan Wallis' wife had told Henry. We caught up with Aunt Judy and talked about the china. Aunt Judy spotted a large teapot at the end of the aisle and moved purposefully ahead.

'There's a letter from a pharmaceutical company employee to his boss, questioning the safety of a drug.'

'What drug?'

'It doesn't say; the employee gives the number.'

'Who was the employee?'

'I don't know, there doesn't seem to be a second page to the letter.' Jim moved away to help Aunt Judy lift the large teapot down from a high shelf. She took one look at the long crack up the back and asked for it to go up there again. She wandered on, looking at the lower shelves. Jim and I lagged behind again. 'There's a note to Gloria, saying he is trying not to put her in danger but the investigation is opening up.'

'Did Gloria ever get that note?'

'I don't think so; it was in a sealed envelope.'

'Then you shouldn't have opened it.'

'Don't you think so?'

'Would you like it if someone opened a letter addressed to you from someone who was very dear to you?'

'No, I suppose not. Should I give it to her?'

Before I could reply, Aunt Judy joined in the conversation. 'Give who what? I went right along that side while you two were stood here chatting. I'll pay for these things and we'll go.'

'I'm sorry, Aunt Judy. Why don't we concentrate on helping you find the antiques you want, and then perhaps Jim could come back to the cottage for a bit?'

Aunt Judy looked at Jim, who raised his eyebrows enquiringly and gave a little lopsided smile.

'I suppose so,' she said, 'on condition he reaches up for those jugs over there!'

I felt slightly unnerved. Jim had charmed my aunt with a cheeky little boy look. He had lied to get on the ward. He had opened a letter not addressed to him. He put his arm around me when I hardly knew him. Was he really interested in all this because he was there when Henry jumped, or was there something else going on?

By the time Jim had gone to get the car to take us back to the cottage, I had told myself I was being silly and he was probably a lovely man who had become intensely interested in the mystery. It was too late to go to the café, even if we had been ready for cream tea. We went back to the cottage and Aunt Judy went straight through to the kitchen to 'rustle up a Victoria sponge'.

'You're honoured,' I said. 'Some guests only get biscuits from the supermarket.'

'I shall thank her very much,' said Jim, 'and it's given us time for me to tell you about the contents of the box file. I've copied you some notes I've made.'

He talked his way through his findings. It certainly looked as if Henry had been very interested in the work of the pharmaceutical company. There were lists of employees and board members, with three circled in red. There was also a list of drugs manufactured there. It was huge. Most of them were crossed off the list, but among the trialled drugs there were three that were underlined.

'I think we are going to tread on some toes if we investigate the drugs firm. Do you think we should carry on?' asked Jim.

'I think we need to find out if any of the drugs completed their trials and if any were seen to have hallucinatory side effects,' I said.

'I don't want to put you or Gloria in danger,' said Jim. 'So I think I ought to look at this on my own.'

'That's very noble of you, but I would like to know the outcome.'

'If it's safe to tell you, I will.'

It felt good to think that Jim was watching out for me. The smell of baking was wafting from the kitchen and I could hear my aunt humming softly. Jim heard her too, and we both smiled, listening. It felt very companionable. Jim moved a little closer to me and was about to say something when Aunt Judy came in with her tray full of warm cake.

'Wow, Judy,' he said, smiling at her, 'this looks wonderful. Do you treat all your guests like this?'

My aunt returned his smile and laughed. Yet I felt uneasy. It was then that I remembered Stephen. How was Jim able to spend all this time with us when he was a full-time carer?

I tried to swallow my doubts about him as I took the plate from my aunt and concentrated on enjoying the soft, warm cake.

27

Jim stayed until seven o'clock. Most of his attention was taken up with talking to Aunt Judy, who embarrassed me dreadfully by telling him first about my childhood and then about my quick promotion to chief librarian. 'Then she left her job to look after my brother, did she tell you?'

I was squirming by then.

Jim answered, 'No, she didn't.' He smiled at me. I managed a half-hearted smile back.

'Then almost as soon as my brother died, my sister-in-law started going a bit doolally. She nursed her too, you know.'

I needed to get out of the room. I gathered up the tea things and went to wash them up. Jim and Aunt Judy were in earnest conversation. I waited until I heard them laugh about something and went back in. I imagined Aunt Judy had probably given up extolling my virtues.

Jim looked up. 'Sorry, Jenny, did we upset you?'

I shrugged. 'I thought I'd better get on with the washing up.'

'Sorry, I could have helped.'

'Nonsense,' said Aunt Judy. 'You are our guest.'

I don't think the 'our' was lost on either Jim or myself. We exchanged a smile.

'But I've probably outstayed my welcome,' said Jim, glancing at his watch. 'Anyway, I'd better get back for Stephen.'

'Where has he been today?' I asked

'On his work experience from college. He has been promoted to help stack shelves in the supermarket. He likes to tell everyone he works there.'

'Who takes him home?'

'The college provides transport. They'll have dropped him off at about six o'clock and my neighbour will have let him in the house. He's okay on his own for an hour or so.'

I chided myself for my earlier doubts. 'You really must say if any of this is interfering with your time with him.'

'I will, don't you worry. I usually get up to date with accounts and tax and stuff now the café is closed for the winter, so that's what I'm avoiding. But I'd better call a cab and hurry back.'

'No, don't worry. I'll take you.'

While I went upstairs for my coat I was still questioning in my mind whether I had fallen for his charm. I couldn't quite rid myself of doubts about him. I wondered if it was always like this for people when they first got to know each other. I certainly didn't know much about relationships.

Jim drove on the way to his house. He got out and I wriggled over to the driver's seat. He leant down to talk to me through the window he had opened before getting out. That felt a bit odd. I wondered whether I was making everything strange. Before he had a chance to say anything, the front door of his house opened. A young man stood there. He called out, 'Dad Jim, is that you?'

'Yes, Stephen, I'm coming.' He turned to me and shrugged. 'Looks like I'm needed. I'll ring you in the morning.'

'I'm going to go and see Gloria tomorrow morning.'

'Okay, would you give me a ring when you're back at your aunt's?'

I nodded, and he waved as he went up to Stephen. By the time I'd wound up the window and turned the car round, I saw he had his arm round the boy's shoulders. Jim was pointing towards the car. They both waved as I drove away. My mind was so full of that image as I drove the six miles back to the cottage that I hardly registered that, unusually for me, I was driving in the dark on my own.

Aunt Judy was pleased to see me back at the cottage so soon. 'I thought you'd make an evening of it over there and I'd be on my own again.'

'I'm back, but I am very tired, Aunt Judy. I may not be very good company.'

'That's all right. We can watch television for a while, and if you're up to it we could play Scrabble.'

I don't think she was quite prepared for me to fall asleep as soon as I sat down to watch a natural history programme with her. Even David Attenborough was not enough to keep me alert. She shook me awake soon after nine, offering me hot chocolate and a biscuit. 'Have a nightcap and then go to bed. We'll have our game of Scrabble tomorrow,' she said. She seemed quite accepting of the fact that I'd been rude enough to sleep rather than spend the evening with her. I wondered if even my sleeping presence was enough to make her feel less alone.

To have an early night was a good idea, but the reality was different. The nightcap seemed to have woken me up, so I lay in bed wondering what we were going to do about all the information in Gloria's box file. It looked as if someone in the pharmaceutical company had raised grave concerns about a drug. I wondered whether Jim had discovered whether it was one that was already in circulation or an experimental drug. Was it the very drug that was used to give Henry hallucinations, or make him totally reckless, or was it something else? And did Henry voluntarily take the probably untested drug which killed him? Or was it given to him in a drink, or some other way – a deliberate action by someone else?

It occurred to me that it was necessary to find out more about the villages and the people around here at that time. A little bit of local knowledge could go a long way, if only I knew how to find that out. But local people definitely held the clue. Someone somewhere knew the secret of both Henry's and Dan Wallis' deaths.

28

The next morning I was up early and took a cup of tea in to Aunt Judy. She was already awake, sitting up with her glasses halfway down her nose, engrossed in reading a crime thriller. I broke it gently to Aunt Judy that I would be visiting Gloria again. I did offer to take her with me, but fortunately she declined. She didn't really need to know that Gloria called me her adoptive daughter.

I bought chocolate, tissues and a daily paper for Gloria from the hospital shop. I had thought about going to the supermarket, but my courage to walk from the car park into the shop had left me. So I had parked as close as possible to the hospital and scuttled in under an umbrella, even though it was hardly raining. I was much better than I had been the day before, but I still needed time for my heart to stop its pounding before walking along the lengthy corridors to Gloria's ward.

Gloria's bed was empty, but its clutter of items – a pen, a half-completed crossword, her toilet bag – suggested a recent occupant, so I didn't think she'd be far away. I went up to the desk to ask about her.

'She's back in X-ray, I'm afraid. She shouldn't be long. Why don't you take a seat in the visitors' area?'

I sat down and picked up the *Devon News*. It was a copy from the day before, but it provided me with something to do while I waited. I read through the section on forthcoming local events and found a larger advert proclaiming that a gentleman called Joe Crane was due to speak to the Rotary Club on Saturday week about his ninety years in Spokeham. This was the next village to Jim and very near to where Henry Standish used to live. I wasn't sure if the Rotary Club allowed ladies, but I tore out the advertisement to take to Jim.

When Gloria did get back up on the ward, she was being wheeled by a rather harassed-looking young porter. I heard her say, 'Now, you be careful, don't knock my legs against the wall. Honestly, it would be quicker to walk.'

She was taken directly up to the nurses' desk, and as I gathered up my things ready to join her, her voice boomed across the ward, 'Has my adoptive daughter arrived yet? She promised she'd visit today.'

'I'm here. I've been waiting for you.' Even as I said this I realised I had, once again, become a co-compounder of the deceit that I was her adopted child.

'Well, wheel me back to my bed, dear. I'm tired and I need to have a rest.'

I smiled and took over from the porter, who looked grateful to be relieved of the responsibility.

'What did you say to that porter?' I asked, as Gloria scrambled onto the bed, swinging up her long bare legs with some ease for a lady of her age.

'I only told him he looked a mess and should get his hair cut. He argued that it was fashionable to have it long. So I told him that while fashion was important, being smart while at your place of work was even more important.'

'He didn't look very happy.'

'Probably he wasn't. But I have to say what I believe. Now, tell me what was in that box file that Henry didn't want the police to see.'

I looked around me. The lady in the next bed seemed to be asleep and the bed the other side was empty. In fact, it looked freshly made, as if waiting for a new inhabitant. Nevertheless, I leant forward and spoke quietly. 'There were quite a few letters and notes about a drug company. Did you know of one in the area?'

'Yes, I did. Phoenix something.'

'Phoenix Pharmaceuticals, perhaps?' I didn't know where I came up with that name; perhaps I had seen it somewhere.

'Yes, I think so, dear, although I'm not sure where it was based. Henry went to London quite often; it may have been there.'

It made sense to me that I may have seen the name in London, although I thought that doubtful. Would someone from London come to kill Henry Standish? That seemed too far-fetched. Mind you, everything seemed unlikely, but here I was in Doddington Hospital with an old lady who told everyone I was her daughter. What was outlandish any more?

I hadn't an awful lot to tell Gloria, really, having not yet seen the file. I didn't even tell her that, in case she was upset that Jim had it in his house. I told her that we hadn't been able to go through everything yet, partly because Aunt Judy and I had been out.

'I remember Judy Harris from when she was a little girl. Judy Drake then, of course,' said Gloria.

'Tell me what she was like,' I said.

Gloria was a great storyteller. She remembered my aunt being the naughtiest girl in her class; I doubted that was true. But she could also remember the day Aunt Judy had moved to Jasmine Cottage and how distraught she had been to leave her old house by the common.

'Why did she leave?'

'They wanted it for building land after the war. She and Peter were devastated. The villagers created a bit of a stink, but to no avail. Planning permission came through really quickly.'

'Can you remember which year that was?' I was trying to work out whether that was anywhere near the time when Henry died.

'No, sorry, dear. You'll have to ask your aunt.'

Gloria and I spent another half-hour or so finishing her crossword and working together on the other puzzles in the paper I had bought her. She had a sharp mind, and often thought of the answers before I did. I could remember times like this with my own mother, although she had died much younger than Gloria was now.

I left Gloria at about eleven forty-five. It wasn't raining, so getting outside was more difficult without using an umbrella. I walked around inside the entrance several times, as if I were waiting for someone. I used all the self-talk that Mike had taught me. Finally, I gave up for the time being and walked into the canteen to buy myself a coffee. I was frightened my anxiety would overwhelm me, but gently calmed myself.

By the time I finished my coffee, I was so irritated with myself at being so pathetic that my anger drove me out of the door to stride across the car park.

29

Gloria's questions about the contents of the box file had started a lot of queries in my mind. Why hadn't I seen it? Jim could have invited me in yesterday when I had taken him home, but that didn't happen. Was he hiding those contents from me, only telling me about the ones that he was happy to share? Or was there really nothing else in there that was important? I decided to call round on the way back to the cottage, to suggest it was my turn to see the box.

I drew up outside Jim's house. I didn't know what to do. I didn't feel quite brave enough to go up to the front door. While I was deliberating, Stephen came out of the house, closely followed by Jim. I wound down the window and called to them.

'Hello, Jenny, what are you doing here?' asked Jim.

I tried not to focus on the fact that he hadn't even asked me how I was. 'I wondered if I might have the box file.'

'Well, you can, but the contents are spread all over the study. I'll walk up to the bus stop with Stephen, and then I'll be back. Do you want to wait indoors?'

My hands were frozen already; it was too cold to stay in the car. 'If you'd help me into your house that would be good.'

Jim opened the car door and put out his hand. I didn't want to hold hands in front of Stephen, so I took hold of the sleeve of Jim's jacket as I stepped out and then tucked my arm through his. I couldn't think whether this looked worse or better, but Stephen didn't seem to notice. He was watching a car a little way along the road.

'Who's that?' he asked Jim.

'I don't know,' said Jim. 'Probably a holidaymaker who's got lost.'

'Here yesterday,' said Stephen, 'Y162...' He screwed up his nose and eyes, trying to remember.

'That's interesting, Stephen. Well spotted,' said Jim.

I looked at the car. It seemed familiar. It turned in the cul-de-sac then drove off as the three of us watched it. Jim took me into the house. Stephen was still outside.

'I don't know who that was, Jenny, but nobody comes up this road by mistake. It's too far off the beaten track. Lock the door behind me and check the back doors are locked; only as a precaution, but we'd better be careful.'

With that, his lips brushed my cheek before he half-ran to catch up with Stephen.

This was the first time I had been in Jim's house. It was cosy. I peeped into room after room, trying to find the study. The sitting room contained three sofas and many books, with little room left for anything else. I hadn't really thought of Jim as a bookish person, so this surprised me. I began to wonder what he had given up to become Stephen's carer.

There was some good artwork on the walls – brilliant colours and some still life drawings. I particularly liked one of the sea. I wondered where he had bought them. I wasn't terribly well up on art and didn't know any modern artists.

I wandered into the kitchen. Everything was neat and tidy, but the kitchen looked even older than mine. I needn't have worried about my house seeming old-fashioned; Jim's was worse. It looked as if he hadn't bought any new furniture for ages. The kitchen was large, though, obviously an extension to the cottage, with space enough for a good-sized pine table and an assortment of chairs around it. Through an open door from the kitchen I could see a desk covered with papers, so concluded that was Jim's study.

I stepped in, feeling like I was intruding. But the box file was there, and as soon as I glanced at the papers, it was obvious that the contents were all over the desk. There were two neat piles on an adjacent table too, with some lines highlighted. I couldn't wait for Jim to get back to tell me what he had discovered already.

I sat on his adjustable chair and began to read papers at random, being careful to put each one back where I had found it.

The drug company certainly featured a great deal. I realised that some of the papers contained whole lines that had been highlighted before being photocopied. Who had given Henry these papers? Was it a whistle-blower? I wondered whether we had a note somewhere about the workplace of Dan Wallis, the other man who had jumped. I couldn't remember whether Henry had known him. If so, perhaps he had given Henry copies of his findings before he died.

I took from my handbag the notebook I had been carrying in case I had to pretend to be a writer. I started some notes, unlabelled, in case they ever reached the wrong hands. First, from where did the papers originate? Was there any clue in the box? For some items it was clear. There was a neat hand-drawn graph with many drugs itemised. This one had been initialled with a clear C. W., not D. W. Did Dan Wallis have any living relatives? If so, had Jim contacted them, or did he think we should? As I looked at all the information spread out before me, my brain was firing with questions and my notes became longer and longer.

There was a noise of a key turning in the lock. I realised I had forgotten to bolt the door. I stepped behind the study door and froze. My heart was pounding loudly and I was scarcely breathing.

'Jenny, where are you?'

My breath escaped audibly and I stepped out from behind the door. Jim jumped as he saw me. 'You didn't bolt the door,' he said.

'No, I got engrossed in this lot.' I waved my hand across the piles of papers.

'I hope you haven't reordered them. It might not look as if I knew what I was doing, but I had a system.' Jim's smile showed me he would not have been incredibly angry if I had reorganised everything.

'I thought of that; they are still in the same groups. Do you know where all these ones from the pharmaceutical company came from?'

'It looks like the work of an insider to me,' said Jim. 'I'm working on the assumption that it was probably Dan Wallis.'

'Have you found anything to suggest Henry knew Dan?'

'Not specifically, but on some of the photocopied documents Henry has written "as sent to station source D. W.?" Henry seemed to think he was the whistle-blower.'

We looked at each other, probably thinking the same thing. If Dan and Henry had both been killed, what would happen to us?

'It was fifty years ago,' said Jim.

'Some people could still be alive. We are stirring things up.'

'We could stop now and go back to ordinary life,' said Jim.

'Or we could find out the truth,' I said, surprising myself. Now I had seen all these papers, my curiosity was definitely aroused.

'I don't want to put you in any danger, Jenny.'

I nearly said the same back to him. Despite my doubts about Jim, I couldn't bear the thought of something happening to him.

'I have a plan,' I said. 'I think we should lie low for several weeks. I should go back to London, perhaps with some of the papers to look at, and you could stay here. But don't talk to anyone about this at all.'

'What about Gloria?'

'Gloria's given me a cover story, hasn't she? I can pop back and see her perhaps once more before I go back to

London, as her adopted daughter. I can give her a get well card with 'Dear Mum' on it, with a bunch of flowers.'

'Do you think she's in danger, now we are involved?'

'I don't know, Jim. You don't think anything sinister was happening to her with that cough and her comatose state, do you?'

'Probably not: she is very old. But we could see if we can get her away for a while. I'll find out if she has anyone to stay with for a few weeks. For convalescence, or while she has central heating fitted, or something.'

'Jim, she might not have a few weeks. She probably has lung cancer.'

'She's so feisty, I forgot.'

I realised we were whispering. I wondered if Jim's home was bugged – or was I being overdramatic?

I mouthed to him that there might be a bug. He didn't hear. I tried again. He was mouthing, 'What?' so I went right up to him and whispered in his ear. He scribbled on a piece of paper, *Could be, I had a creepy crawly in my bed last night!* I wrote, *I am being serious!* Jim stopped smiling and wrote, *Sorry. I don't think so. I will have a bit of a search about to check, but meanwhile let's pretend we are really good friends and chat about anything.*

So we did. I asked him about his books and found out that he had been doing an Open University course, but then when he took on Stephen he decided he would have to give it up; he wouldn't be able to manage with studying, running the café and bringing up a child when he had never been a father before,

'Are you thinking of doing OU again, some day?' I asked.

'Perhaps not OU, but more education, probably. The plan for Stephen is that he will go into a staffed hostel with other youngsters as a step towards independent living. Plus I'll have more time when I retire, anyway.'

'So what would have been your dream occupation?'

'Art therapist.'

'Oh, that explains the collection of art on the walls. You have an eye for a good picture. Who painted the still life on your sitting room wall?'

'I did.'

I looked at him in amazement. I went into his sitting room, and he followed me. I started pointing at the pictures, saying each time, 'This one?'

There was only one response: 'Mine.'

I went through to the hall. 'This one?'

Jim laughed. 'That, my dear, is a Turner! A print, of course!'

'Oh, yes, so it is!'

'I must take you to some art galleries, if you'd like to go. It would be lovely to spend time looking at pictures.'

'Once I can get there.'

'You'll be able to, soon. Think what you have achieved in the last few days.'

I smiled as I raised my eyebrows. I loved the way Jim encouraged me. I was feeling so relaxed in his company. Strangely, my doubts about him were dispelled by the fact that we both felt in danger. Or did I? In some ways I felt safer with Jim than I had ever felt.

'I'll miss you when I go back to London,' I said.

Jim took both my hands in his. 'I miss you every time you leave my side.'

I felt myself colour up. I smiled at Jim, but gently pulled my hands away from his. I gradually drew my eyes away from him and patted at my hair. I found myself wondering what my psychologist would say about all this. Thinking of Mike made me realise that I hadn't contacted him.

'Jim, I need to get in touch with Mike Lewis. I've sort of disappeared, from his point of view. I ought to update him.'

Jim sighed. 'Use my computer and send him an email. I'll make you a cup of tea while you do it. I presume you have his email address. Do you know how to get to your emails from a different computer?'

'No, you'll have to show me. And yes, the email address is on the appointment letter in my handbag.'

I sat there for a few moments after he had helped me reach my emails. Jim was running water into the kettle, and that simple act sounded good. I started to write to my psychologist:

> *Dear Mike*
> *I thought I would update you with how I am. All my negative beliefs are being challenged and I feel my life is turning around. Jim is a really positive person and I think that with God's help, I can be like that too. I am excited about life again, even though we are uncovering one or two mysteries.*
> *My findings so far have been interesting in that we think that the suicide I saw from a beach in my childhood was not a suicide at all, because it was a detective who died when working on a case involving a drug company. However, this means I am in great danger, as is Jim. I think I am being*

followed and that Jim's place may be bugged. It makes it difficult for me to know who to trust. I have tried to explain this to Jim, but I don't know if he considers it is in my imagination. I've copied this to Jim too and I don't mind if you speak to him.

Jim had come back with tea in a flowery mug. I briefly wondered what other ladies he entertained. He was frowning as he glanced at my email. He whispered, 'You are being careful what you write, Jenny, aren't you? Not that I think anyone would hack into your emails, but I prefer to think of them as open postcards, which is what I was taught at the library computing skills course I went on.'

'Oh dear. I didn't realise.'

Jim leaned over my shoulder and began to read, mumbling, 'May I?' I felt strangely embarrassed as he read, even though I had intended to send him a copy.

'How about taking out the bit about the beach episode and adding in something about details of your childhood? Then you can say about Gloria being known to you when you were a child and lived round here. Your psychologist would probably like to know the reason why you called on her.'

I was about to argue with him that it wasn't true, when I realised he had said the last sentence loud enough for any bug to pick up.

I changed the last sentence to the first paragraph and rewrote the rest. My new draft didn't read quite as coherently, but it was more like something that could be read by anyone.

My findings so far have been interesting in tracking people I may have known as a child, including a lady called Gloria, who we visited on the way. Gloria may be the person who took me for my first aid Guide badge. Unfortunately Gloria is ill in hospital – we found her in quite a state with bronchitis, so what she taught me all those years ago was useful in helping her.

However, I can't shrug off the feeling that I am being followed for some reason and I think Jim's place may be bugged. This is quite frightening and makes it difficult for me to know who to trust. Jim thinks I am imagining it. I don't mind if you email him.

I'm not sure when I'm coming back, but I'll try to keep my appointment next week.

I signed off. As I pressed 'send', I picked up the flowery mug of tea and quickly drank it, aware of the time. 'I'd best go now, Jim. Aunt Judy expected me back at the cottage for a late lunch.'

'Sorry, I've embarrassed you.'

'No, no. I genuinely have to go.'

Jim put his arm round me to give me a soft, brief kiss on my lips. I stayed there a moment before pulling away. 'Aren't we a bit old for this, Jim?' I tried to sound casual as I put on my coat and picked up my handbag.

I turned to look at him. He was looking straight at me, and as I thought again what gentle eyes he had, I waited to hear what he was trying to say. 'Sometimes life doesn't seem to take notice of age. I don't feel too old to spend time with such a lovely lady. All I feel is blessed. Come on, I'll see you to your car.'

30

When I arrived at Jasmine Cottage, I expected to be met by a rather tetchy Aunt Judy. But quite the contrary: she had been waiting for me to arrive and had laid a lovely lunch on the dining room table. She seemed very excited to see me. 'You're famous, Jenny. I've had a reporter round to ask all about you.'

My heart sank. I immediately became wary. 'Who was he, Aunt Judy, and how did you know he was a reporter? You should never let anyone in the house.'

'He said he was a reporter from the *Devon News*. He showed me an ID card. And he knew your name. Seemed to think you were Gloria's adopted daughter, though, so I put that right!'

'Gloria calls me her adopted daughter because of what I've done for her.'

'Oh, does she? I'm not sure she has the right to do that!'

I was about to apologise, but Aunt Judy carried on telling me about the reporter. 'I told him you lived in London and you used to be a chief librarian and that you'd looked after your mum and dad before they died. He was most interested to know where you lived. I didn't tell him the address; I said he'd have to ask you himself.'

'Did you say whereabouts in London?'

'I couldn't think. I said it was Tottenham Road.'

Thankfully, I don't live in Tottenham Road. I don't know where she conjured up that name.

'Did he ask about Gloria at all? Or anything else?'

'He asked how you knew Jim. But I didn't tell him about you on the beach. I said you'd met one time when you were staying here. It wasn't really something to boast about, that you panicked.'

'That's good, Aunt Judy. I don't want it all in the paper. In fact, I don't want *anything* in the paper.'

'I told him you'd say that, so he's coming back at four o'clock to talk it through with you.'

'What? I think I'd better be out. I really don't want to talk to a reporter, if that's what he is.'

'I think he is, dear. He's like the photo in the paper.'

'Show me.'

Aunt Judy rummaged through the pile of old newspapers she kept by the fire. She tutted as she went, muttering to herself, 'It's here somewhere, not there, not there,' as she went through. Then, 'Aha! Here it is. That's him.'

There was a photo next to an article by 'Tom Henderson, *Devon News* reporter'. It was dated about two months before.

'I don't want people poking their noses into my business,' I told my aunt. 'I'm a private person.'

'But you and Jim did a very special thing.'

'No, we were there when we were needed, that's all.'

'Well, he's coming at four, so you can tell him not to write anything then.'

All through lunch I was wondering what to do. I needed to talk to Jim. Despite him teasing me, I still thought it was a very real possibility that his phone might be bugged. I wondered if I could give him a coded message, or even alert him by telling him that a reporter was coming and exactly what my aunt had already told him.

I could hardly eat – the meal seemed to drag on endlessly. As soon as she started to clear away, I said to Aunt Judy that I had to get one or two things from the shop in the next village. I wasted no time in setting off in the car. I was really looking for a phone box. I had worked out what I would say to Jim and how I would say it. I really hoped he would be in.

I put my coins in and rang the number. His voice answered and I pressed the button for the money to go through. This seemed like a really old-fashioned phone box compared with the ones in London.

'Hello, Jim.'

'Jenny, how wonderful. I was thinking about you.'

I smiled at the thought that he might have been. 'You old charmer! Enough of that nonsense. I am ringing with a purpose!'

'Sorry, but it is true. I was thinking about you.'

'Listen for a minute! I'm ringing to tell you that a reporter called round to talk to Aunt Judy today.'

There was the merest of pauses before Jim said, 'Oh, that's interesting. What was it about?'

'You and me, actually. It seems we are some sort of heroes for calling the ambulance for Gloria.'

Again, a slight pause. 'Are we? I suppose she told him all about it?'

'Well, more or less. I don't really fancy being in the paper, do you?'

'No, not really, Jen. We happened to call in on your friend and found her ill, end of story. It's not particularly newsworthy, is it?'

'I wouldn't have thought so. But he's coming back to talk to me at four o'clock today, so it occurred to me that it would be only polite to tell you, since it was both of us there and I shall probably have to talk about you too.'

'Well, that's kind of you, dear. I suppose it wouldn't have been much fun to see my name in the paper if I didn't know. I was going to see you this evening... Do you think I should come over earlier, so that I'm there when he is?'

'No, it's fine. I'll tell him to ring you if he wants to talk to you too.'

'It's lovely to have some time together while you're in Devon. Have you decided when you're going back?'

'I have an appointment on Thursday, so I'll need to be home by then.'

'That's a real shame, I shall miss you. You'll have to come for longer next time.'

I wondered if I was meant to find some hidden message in what he was saying, but he sounded very genuine. I realised there was a bit of a gap in the conversation. I replied, 'Jim, you are a dear. I shall miss you too. But I haven't gone yet. We'll have a lovely time tonight, I'm sure.'

'You'll love the restaurant. It's my favourite.'

This was news – we were going out tonight. It was all news, actually, as we hadn't planned to meet up at all. I hoped Aunt Judy didn't mind. 'Where are we going? I don't know whether to dress up a bit – you know, borrow Aunt Judy's evening outfit.'

Jim's chortle burbled down the phone. 'I'm not sure you'd look good in one of her outfits. You wear what you like; to me, you always look lovely!'

I didn't know what to say for a moment; I wasn't practised at receiving compliments. 'I'd better go now or I won't be back for this reporter chap, Tom Henderson. I'm out at the moment getting some chocolates as a thank you for Aunt Judy, and a few bits.'

'I wondered why you'd called me on a payphone.'

'It wasn't only that; I thought Aunt Judy wouldn't approve of me ringing you when I'd been late for lunch because I had been with you this morning!'

Realising what I'd said, I wondered how that would seem to him… a woman of my age apparently still under the control of my older relative. But it wasn't only that – it felt so strange to have our friendship observed by Aunt Judy. Jim was chortling. 'You'd better hurry back to your aunt now, or she may not let you out this evening!'

'Don't be such a tease!' I laughed too. 'But it is time I got on.'

'Well, bye for now, my dear. See you later.'

'Bye, dear Jim. Until this evening.'

I put the phone down. At least I had alerted him to the danger. I hoped that if he was being bugged, then the phone call would be innocent enough. Jim had made a really good job of turning our conversation into something romantic, in case someone was listening. I prayed he really meant some of what he said.

31

I arrived back at Jasmine Cottage with a huge bunch of mixed chrysanthemums for Aunt Judy and a large box of chocolates. Chrysanthemums aren't my favourite flowers, but they were all I could find in the small village shop.

'I love the autumn colours,' she said, as she took the bunch from me. She pulled off the paper from around the edge. 'Lovely strong stems – they should last well.' She reached up to give me a quick hug and bustled away to find a vase.

I took my outdoor clothes upstairs to the little guest room. I hung my coat on the back of the door, then opened the wardrobe. I had brought very little with me to go out in, only one soft blue, Merino wool, knee-length dress. It was a favourite, but old. I wasn't sure about it, but then on the other hand it would probably be fine whether we ended up eating chips somewhere or having a candlelit meal. I stopped myself at that thought and smartly closed the wardrobe door. Such nonsense for a woman of my age!

I went back downstairs and told Aunt Judy that I wouldn't want an evening meal because I was going out this evening. 'I'm not quite sure if Jim meant it, but he said something about showing me a favourite place of his where he liked to eat.'

'Really, Jenny. You shouldn't be so vague. I'm disappointed you won't be here. When are we going to have our game of Scrabble?'

'Now?'

'What about that reporter?'

'We can pause our game and resume it when he's gone. It sounds as if you told him what happened, so I can't think why he's coming.'

'I expect he needs your permission to use the story. He might have written something already for you to look at.'

'Well, I hope not, because I really don't want anything in the paper at all. I'd rather stay out of the limelight.'

We settled down and started on our game. It wasn't long before I was struggling to keep up. Aunt Judy loved words and spent a great deal of her spare time doing crosswords and word games. I was outclassed.

We must have been on about our fifth round when there was a knock at the door.

'I'll get it,' said Aunt Judy. 'It will be the reporter.'

I stood up, feeling nervous. I had never been interviewed by a reporter before. Over these few days I had stepped out of too many comfort zones. I realised I was hugging my arms around me.

The man who came into the room, wearing a dark coat and putting down the hood as he stooped under Aunt Judy's low doorframe, was probably in his early thirties. He looked strangely familiar. Maybe it was because of the picture in the paper.

I swallowed hard as I realised this might be the driver of the car that had turned round by Jim's house. He came towards me, holding out his hand. 'Pleasure to meet you,

Miss Drake.' I managed to unfold an arm to take his hand. It was a strong handshake, but not too gripping.

'Hello,' was all I could manage.

Aunt Judy, ever the perfect hostess, invited him to sit down. He waited for me to sit and then took the chair opposite me. My head was swimming. What did it mean if he was the man we had seen in Jim's road? Was he a genuine reporter? I cleared my throat and pushed myself to speak over Aunt Judy, who was now offering him a cup of tea. 'How do I know you are a genuine reporter?'

'Oh, sorry, my identification. The photo's a bit out of date, but it still looks a bit like me.'

Aunt Judy left the room, muttering about putting the kettle on. I felt very alone. I took the rather battered card and looked at it. It could have been anyone, but the name underneath was 'Tom Henderson'. I would have absolutely no way of knowing if it were genuine. He was leaning forward, looking perturbed.

I handed the ID back to him. 'Sorry, it's only that I thought I'd seen you before somewhere.'

'That's my fault.'

I waited for an explanation. He continued, 'I was going to go to talk to Jim Tyler yesterday. But I saw he was busy.'

'So it was your car that turned round in front of his house?'

'Yes. You all watched me go.'

I remembered Stephen was there. This seemed to be a plausible explanation. I gave a nod and settled back in my seat, observing him.

He pulled a notebook out of his pocket. 'I'll come straight to the point,' he said. I thought I would rather he

213

didn't while Aunt Judy was out of the room, but then decided this was nonsense and I could listen.

'I was interested in how you found Gloria Standish, because I have been concerned about that lady.'

That one sentence turned things right around for me. It was possible that this man had information we needed. 'What do you mean?' I asked as casually as I could, with my heart pounding.

'I thought she might be in danger.'

'Why would she be?'

'I've been intrigued by the circumstances of her husband's death. I've been poking around a bit, and I think I may have disturbed a hornets' nest.'

'A hornets' nest?' I queried.

'I think you and Jim Tyler might unwittingly have stumbled on a few things that might help me.'

I could no longer think straight at all. I was trying to work out whether this young man was a friend or foe, whether he was genuine and being cautious or being wily and manipulative to find out whether we knew anything.

'We found Gloria in her front room in some sort of coma.'

'She may have been drugged.'

I've never been able to play poker or any card game where there was some element of deceit, so my mouth probably hung open at this. 'Why would anyone drug her?' My breath was becoming laboured. I was beginning to panic.

'I'm sorry, I've startled you. I didn't mean to alarm you, although I realised it might. I needed you to know. I'm sorry. I don't want to make you nervous.'

I couldn't really listen; I was trying to sort myself out.

He went to the door. 'Mrs Harris, your niece is not well. I think I've upset her.'

'It's okay, it's okay,' I was trying to say, as I wrestled with trying to find some calming thoughts. 'Give me a minute. Water.'

My aunt had brought water. 'She has these turns sometimes,' she explained to the reporter. She stood by me, gently rubbing my back.

The world was beginning to steady again. I wanted to put my head between my legs, but I couldn't do that in front of the reporter. Nor could I tell him to go away. I concentrated on silently counting my breaths, and things gradually came back to near normal.

'Panic attack. Sorry.'

'Sorry I caused one. I didn't know.'

Aunt Judy moved towards the door, saying, 'I'll go and finish making the tea, and put some sugar in it.'

I turned back to Mr Henderson. 'I am very fond of Gloria. If someone drugged her, will they try to get to her in hospital?'

'I think they know she's harmless now.'

'Why would they think that if they didn't before?' My mind was beginning to work properly. I could look at this objectively now.

'They've found out it isn't her who has been making enquiries about an event that happened more than fifty years ago.'

I realised Aunt Judy was struggling to carry a tray full of teapot, fancy milk jug, sugar bowl, biscuits, plus plates and serviettes. Tom Henderson stood to take it from her and placed it on the table.

'Aunt Judy, please could you fetch me an energy bar? I think it might help. There's one in my handbag upstairs.'

My aunt sped out of the room, obviously glad to have an errand.

I turned to the reporter. 'And do you know who has been making these enquiries?'

'I'm pretty sure it's you and Jim Tyler. You'll have to stop before they come to the same conclusion.'

'This all sounds preposterous.'

My aunt was calling from upstairs. 'Jenny, where did you say?'

I raised my voice to tell her. 'Try my coat pocket, if it's not in my handbag.' I turned to the reporter. 'I don't know about all this. Perhaps you'd better talk to Jim. But what about this piece you're writing?' We could hear my aunt on the stairs.

The reporter leant forward and said, quietly, 'No article; means to an end.'

I looked at him, trying to understand what he meant. Aunt Judy came cautiously into the room, and the reporter continued in a normal voice, 'I can't change your mind about the article?'

Aunt Judy put my energy bar by the cup of tea. I shook my head as the reporter sipped at his tea. He solemnly dunked his biscuit as I answered, 'I really don't think there is much of a story here. I went to see Gloria and found her very ill. It must happen all the time, that sort of thing. I don't think your readers will be at all interested.'

'Well, if you have a change of heart, Miss Drake, please call me. It is exactly the sort of human interest story that people like.' He opened his wallet to extract a small square business card. I took it from him and glanced at it, before slipping it into my own pocket. My hunch had been right: he may have looked at little like Tom Henderson, but he was not the reporter.

Aunt Judy held the fort while he finished having his tea and refused another biscuit. She didn't know he was Graham Clark, private investigator. Luckily, little was required from me. I felt a bit hot and bothered after the panic attack. In fact the whole 'interview' had exhausted me. Aunt Judy's chatter with him about the weather, the village he came from and the newspaper she thought he was writing for wafted around me as I gave a nod here and there or dropped in an odd word. Finally, she took him to the front door. I could hear her saying, 'I think it would make a good story too. I'll see if I can persuade her to change her mind.'

I took stock. A reporter was one thing, but an investigator could be someone on either side, and had he, or had he not, suggested that we leave it all alone?

Meanwhile, Aunt Judy had come back into the room and was still talking about the article. She was not pleased that I had refused to let 'the reporter' run with it.

'But, Aunt Judy, there's nothing to report. We called round because she sounded ill when I spoke to her on the phone, that's all.'

'It was a jolly good thing you did, because she probably wouldn't have made it through the night if you had come straight here. Which is why that strange young man wanted a story.'

I laughed. I nearly showed her his business card, but thought I'd better not. I was dying to have another look at the photo of the reporter in the paper; he had certainly convinced my aunt that he was Tom Henderson. But meanwhile, I had the rest of the evening to think about. It was already gone five o'clock and I had no idea what time Jim would come round. My aunt was bringing over the small table with the half-finished Scrabble game.

'Do you mind if we finish our game tomorrow? I need to have a bit of a freshen-up at least and maybe a rest before I go out with Jim.'

As soon as I said it, I realised that this was, in fact, a date. Was this genuine, or part of the subterfuge? Nothing seemed to make sense any more. A friend who pretended to be more, but might be; a reporter who revealed he was not who he said by giving me a different business card; a phone that might be bugged; and the suspicion that Gloria had been drugged, maybe with the intention of killing her.

I needed some time to myself.

I couldn't manage a lie-down; my mind was working too fast. I had a bath and that relaxed me a little, then I went to the wardrobe and surveyed the blue dress again. It would have to do. I slipped it on, then changed my mind and tried my pair of black trousers and a jumper. I felt too ordinary, so once again I put on the dress and found tights to go with it.

'You look nice dear,' said Aunt Judy when I eventually went downstairs. 'I have a lovely floaty scarf that would go beautifully with that dress. Would you like to borrow it?'

We went upstairs and she pulled a drawer right out of her bow-fronted chest of drawers and emptied the contents onto the bed. There must have been more than fifty scarves. She pulled the end of one to reveal the most beautiful peacock design. I took it from her and turned to the mirror to look as I looped it round my neck. The long ends hung nearly to the hem of the dress, making me look taller.

'It's beautiful, Aunt Judy. Thank you so much.'

My aunt's eyes had welled up. She sniffed. At that moment, I realised how important I was to her. 'You keep the scarf, dear. I don't have the right colours for it these days, and it really suits your eyes.'

There was a knock on the front door. I gave Aunt Judy a hug before she went to answer it. After a few minutes she called up, 'Jim's here, Jenny. Are you nearly ready?'

I took my coat from the back of the bedroom door and went down the stairs. Jim was at the bottom, and he smiled up at me. 'You look incredible,' he said.

He didn't look too bad himself. I hadn't seen him in a suit before. I was really pleased I had put on a decent dress. 'I had no idea where we were going, so it was pot luck, really, as to what I put on,' I said. 'But I'm glad I'm nearly as smart as you!'

Jim smiled as he took my coat and held it for me as I put it on. Aunt Judy was beaming at us both. I wondered if she had ever had anyone interested in her since Uncle Peter had died. I hadn't thought much about her as a widow for many years, but it was good to feel closer to her. I gave her a quick kiss as we left, Jim's arm around my shoulders.

But I thought to myself that it was a real shame that this was, in effect, a business meal. We two amateur detectives would have to discuss the pseudo-reporter's visit and whether or not we could trust him with what we had found. Perhaps one day we would be able to simply focus on us.

32

We walked arm in arm to my hired car. I made a mental note to ring in the morning to extend the hire for a day or two. We pulled away from the cottage, waving to Aunt Judy who was still stood surrounded by light in her hall, watching us as we left. Of course, she couldn't see me waving. I felt guilty that I hid so many secrets from her, but we were into the investigation too far to back off now. I started to talk to Jim about the reporter's visit on the way to the restaurant.

'The reporter isn't a reporter; he's a private detective,' I told him, 'even though, according to my aunt, he looks similar to one of the journalists for the local paper.'

'I know. He came to see me as well. Hang on a minute; I'll pull over.'

He pulled into the next lay-by and switched off the engine and the lights. It seemed very dark, apart from the occasional sweep of headlights as they came up round the bend behind us or approached and disappeared on the other side of the road.

'What did he say to you?' I asked.

'He was quite open. I was the only one in the house, and at first I wouldn't let him in because I recognised the car, so he introduced himself as a reporter and showed me his ID with his real business card at the same time.'

'You didn't talk in the house, did you?' I asked, thinking of our fears about the place being bugged.

'No, I didn't. I told him I was on my way to visit someone at the other end of the village and would be walking rather than going in the van. So he said perhaps he could come another time, and then we walked up the road together to nowhere in particular.'

'You thought he was genuine, then?'

'As genuine as someone pretending he was someone else! I didn't know if I could trust him, but I wanted to hear what he had to say. I thought I was safer outside where we couldn't be overheard.'

'So what did he say?' My heart was racing.

'Not much more than he told you, I think. He was afraid that Gloria had been drugged. He said you'd had a panic attack when he told you. He seemed quite upset about that. He had thought anyone who was brave enough to be investigating Henry's death would be able to cope.'

'I did cope. I merely had a panic attack from the shock.'

'I know, my dear, I know.'

'Jim, don't, you're confusing me.'

'Don't what?'

'Call me "my dear" in that way, when you don't have to pretend we are more of a couple than we are.'

Jim looked at me. A car swept by and I could see from his expression that he did not understand. I tried to return his gaze, but my eyes filled up and I had to look down. Immediately he leant towards me and gently put his hand under my chin so that I had to look at him while he spoke.

'Jenny, listen. I really enjoy your company and I have become very fond of you. I call you "my dear" because it comes naturally out of how I feel. If you don't like it, I'll try to stop. Already I want to call you "darling"; I have to hold myself back to say "my dear"!'

The silence in the car felt full of expectation. I wanted to say something, but I couldn't do anything other than look at him. Jim seemed to misinterpret my blankness; he took his hand away from my chin and looked away. I wanted to hang on to that beautiful moment. I found my voice. 'You want to call me "darling"?'

He looked at me as he replied. 'Yes. Always.'

I couldn't pull my eyes away from his. I didn't know if there was any way I could respond. I was fifty-five and someone wanted to call me 'darling'. I'd had a boyfriend in my late teens who had called me 'darling', until my friend became jealous and started flirting with him. But no one else had called me that other than my mother, whose 'darling' had eventually become a universal name for all those whom she vaguely recognised, as she became more confused.

I forced myself to speak. 'You can call me "darling" whenever you like.'

'Always?'

'You may always call me "darling"… until you want to save the name for someone else.'

'Phew! That's always, then.'

I laughed. A laugh I could hardly control. It came up from within me and felt as if it filled my whole being. Jim took both my hands in his, his wonderful solid hands completely enclosing mine. We leant towards each other and he gently kissed me on my lips. A soft, beautiful kiss that I felt as if I had been waiting for forever.

Jim leant back in the driver's seat. 'We need to be able to sit and talk somewhere else,' he said. 'I so want you in my arms. Let's sort out what we are doing about Graham Clark and whether we trust him, and then go and have that lovely meal in Brankside. They have some settees in the corner by an open fire, and couples often sit there while they wait for their table.'

'Fine by me,' I said, in response to his first suggestion. Sitting very close on a settee in front of other people felt rather public. 'Do you trust Graham? I have no idea who to trust these days. I didn't even trust you for a while.'

'Do you trust me now?'

'Now I know that you aren't pretending to like me, I think I do.'

'We'll discuss that word "like" later! But we must concentrate on sorting out what to do next regarding our mystery.' Reluctantly, I nodded in agreement. Jim continued, 'I think I trust Graham. He says he has been investigating this for a few years. When he went into the library in Flyncombe a few weeks ago, the librarian, who he knows quite well, told him that there had been other enquiries about Henry Standish.'

'That was us.'

'Yes, it was. He traced me easily. But it took some further digging to work out who you were and how you were involved, until you came to Devon to see Aunt Judy. Then he heard who it was who found Gloria, so that was it, really – he had all the information he needed to track us down.'

'Does he know anything more?'

'He's pretty sure that Gloria was drugged. I don't think he managed to tell you that he has identified three people who were working on some experimental drugs in the pharmaceutical company. Some of those drugs went missing not long before Dan leapt off that bridge. There was a great hoo-ha about the missing drugs before the management decided that they must have been disposed of by mistake.'

'What were the drugs for?'

'They were sleeping tablets, but they were never manufactured because of their strong hallucinogenic qualities.'

'Don't tell me, they found people thought they could fly.'

'Precisely. They heightened the senses to the extent that the user felt as if they could do anything, including flying. Coupled with a dreamy sleepy feeling, they were incredibly dangerous.'

'How many more of these drugs are missing?'

'Probably as many as eight doses.'

I felt a shiver run down my back. Jim spoke again. 'Don't think about it, Jenny. They're very unlikely to still be around. I think we were overreacting the other day when we began to think we are in danger. The researchers are probably all dead by now, or very old. And I don't think Gloria was drugged – she was already ill when you spoke to her on the phone.'

I nodded. What he said made sense, but I was still frightened.

Jim took my hand and kissed it. 'We can always back out, you know.'

'I don't know. What about Gloria? She needs to know.'

Jim nodded briefly and started the engine. We drove in silence to the restaurant. Jim took my arm as I got out of the car and I clung to him, not to calm my panic at being outside, but because I never wanted to be without him.

Inside, we were shown through to the small lounge. It was a beautiful, huge room, with a fire at each end. The one at the far end had a screen behind a settee, presumably to stop a draught, and looked completely isolated. After our coats were taken, Jim took my hand and we walked over to it. Together we sat down and Jim's arm went round my shoulders, pulling me closer. I leant against him and felt him kiss the top of my head. I turned towards him more so that I could rest my arm on his chest. Slightly hidden from general view, we sat there, being with each other. I felt so safe, so sure of him, I didn't care if anyone saw, and didn't move when our drinks were placed discreetly on a low table beside us.

'I want to always be part of your life,' said Jim. 'From that day when you arrived in my café I have wanted to look after you.'

'You were wonderful that day.' I didn't really want to speak about it. I simply wanted to be here, in the moment.

'I longed to take you in my arms. Isn't this beautiful?'

'Mmm.'

I've never been so pleased to wait more than half an hour for a table. The waiter did appear a couple of times, but when he saw our unfinished drinks he melted away again. Finally, Jim said, 'I think we'd better go and eat.'

We picked up our hardly touched drinks to take through. I realised Jim had probably been sending the waiter away. Then the misgivings came: had he brought other women here? He hadn't booked a bedroom, had he? I tried to push the doubts away.

'They seem to know you here. Have you been before?'

'We often come on a Sunday after church, Stephen and I. They are wonderful with him. But they always take us straight to our table – over there, that one,' he pointed to the furthest corner where the table was partly obscured by the shape of the room. 'Stephen hasn't the best table manners, so I asked for that table the first time we came and it has become our regular place.'

'So haven't you been in the evening before?'

'Only once, with some relatives, on my sixtieth birthday.'

'How old are you, then?'

'I'm sixty-one, you missed the great day by a year.'

I sat there thinking about all the times we had missed. I would have loved to have had him by my side when I was nursing my parents, especially my mother. It was so hard with someone who could no longer remember you were her daughter.

'Penny for your thoughts, my darling.'

It sounded so strange, and so right. I looked at Jim. 'I was thinking about all the times and people we've missed. So many birthdays, my parents, your sister, me as a chief librarian. Everything.'

'No, not everything. We're here now, and I know your Aunt Judy and Stephen knows you, or will do soon. He

227

already knows who you are. You'll be there for my seventieth and I shall be there for your fiftieth.'

'Too late – I've had it. I'm fifty-five.'

'In that case, you'll have to tell me all about it.'

'My fiftieth? Nothing much to tell, except Aunt Judy arrived with a cake and champagne and we both got tiddly over a game of Scrabble which she let me win!'

'Sounds better than mine. Stephen went missing from school – no one knows how he got through the gate. The police found him eventually at about ten in the evening. I was worried out of my mind.'

'You've done a good job with him.'

'Sometimes I've done it wrong. I've had to pray hard that things would turn out for the best. I think it would have been beyond me otherwise. I'm pleased he's come on as far as he has.'

I sat there thinking how different his faith was from mine. It seemed as if I didn't have a belief in the same God. He prayed as if to a friend. Apart from the last few days, I could only think of God as noticing all my wrongdoings.

I glanced at Jim, thinking how lucky I was to be with such a caring man. I tried a little prayer of thanks with a request that I wasn't being duped and that he understood how difficult life was for me. 'I think you've done well. I couldn't have coped.'

'But I couldn't have coped with nursing my parents. Nor not being able to go out and having those panic attacks.'

'I didn't even feel near to a panic attack coming in here today.'

'That must be because we were arm in arm. Use my arm any time you need to!'

'I won't have you there in London.'

'Remind me why you live there.'

'I'm not sure. I always have, since we moved from Devon when I was ten years old. Is that a reason? The house is full of memories of my parents – some good ones, but the bad ones too. Both my parents have died there…'

Jim interrupted, 'Are there any reasons why you are still there that are not connected to past history?'

I thought for a bit. 'The only one, really, is my psychologist, Mike Lewis. He has helped me a great deal. I was totally housebound when I first saw him. I wouldn't have been visiting here if it hadn't been for him.'

'So you're staying in your house in London because of your meetings with your psychologist. How often are they?'

'They used to be weekly, but they're about every fortnight now and he is reducing them as I make progress.'

'Then you could move here to live, if you wanted to.'

I considered this for a few moments before I answered. 'Oh, I don't know about that. It sounds like too big a change.'

'It's only a thought. If you and I want to be together more, we'll have to work out how to do it.'

I was feeling a bit uncomfortable. 'Don't let's talk about it tonight; it's too soon.'

'Jenny, my darling, we don't have to talk about it at all, if you don't want to.'

I smiled at him, feeling a little more relaxed. I was only just beginning to absorb that Jim and I might be together forever.

'How's the salmon?' Jim asked.

'Delicious,' I replied.

His boyish grin showed how extremely pleased he was about us being there, in his favourite place to eat. I settled down to enjoy the meal, and his company.

33

When we arrived back at Aunt Judy's it was around ten o'clock. I suggested to Jim that it would be good to see if my aunt were up and, if so, for him to say goodnight to her. He gave me a hug and we kissed on the doorstep before going into the cottage.

As we went into the front room, we disturbed Aunt Judy, who was snoozing in front of the television. She jumped as she woke up. I went over and bent down by her chair to speak to her. 'I'm sorry we woke you, Aunt Judy. Jim wanted to say goodnight before he went.'

'Goodnight? What do you mean "goodnight"? What time is it?'

'Ten o'clock, just gone.'

'It's not late enough for him to go home. Jenny, make us all an evening drink.'

I smiled at Jim, who shrugged his shoulders. He came forward and took the seat opposite Aunt Judy, who immediately requested a full account of our meal. By the time I came back with two hot chocolates and a coffee for Jim, she had arranged to take Jim and me to try the midweek lunch menu at Brankside.

'It will be my treat,' she said. 'I haven't taken Jenny anywhere decent for lunch this visit. You've monopolised her completely!'

'I'm so sorry, Mrs Harris. I didn't mean to – well, not all the time.'

We exchanged glances surreptitiously, but nothing seemed to get past Aunt Judy.

'Seems to me that you two have greatly enjoyed each other's company. No bad thing; I'd hate to get in the way of your...' she paused long enough for us to see she was fishing for the word, '... friendship.'

'It would be lovely to go to lunch with you, Aunt Judy. Thank you for inviting us both.'

'Doesn't look as if it would be right to invite one without the other. Stop looking at me like that, Jenny, and drink your hot chocolate.'

Feeling like a small child with an all-knowing mother, I did as I was told. Jim was trying not to laugh.

Jim didn't stay too long. He did give me a hug as he went, but thankfully no kiss in front of my aunt! I was already feeling like a naughty teenager. I knew that as soon as the door was closed I would be subjected to many questions. I was right.

'What do you think about Jim, then, Jenny? Is he the man for you? At your age you shouldn't be playing around, and nor should he.'

'I don't think we're "playing around", Aunt Judy. We are both growing fond of each other.'

'I thought you'd always be a spinster now you've been one so long. You surprise me, Jenny. I might have to be funding a wedding yet.'

I laughed. The very thought of a wedding seemed like a fantasy. 'I had rather thought marriage had passed me by.'

My aunt made a noise that sounded rather like a horse snorting. I wondered why older people felt they could say exactly what they liked and get away with it. I cleared away the cups and went to wash up.

It was while I was washing up that I realised my aunt had said she would fund my wedding. I still didn't think there would be one, but it made me feel really good to know that I was so important to her.

When I went back into the room, she was plumping up cushions on the old settee. I gave her a hug.

'What's that for?' she asked.

'For being you and caring about what happens to me. Thank you.'

'I often wish you lived nearer, dear. I'd love to see more of you.'

I woke in the morning determined to check up on Gloria. I was still a bit worried about someone trying to slip her a drug, despite the fact that Graham seemed to think that if anyone was a target, we were. I wondered if Jim had told Graham about the box file. I had forgotten to ask Jim if he had discovered anything further of interest when he was looking through it.

I wanted to talk to Jim more than anything. I couldn't think about him without becoming all tingly. I wondered if that was normal for a woman of my age.

It was only seven-thirty when I ate my breakfast on my own. I then boiled an egg for Aunt Judy and took it up to her with two thin slices of brown toast. She sat up as soon as I entered her room, and a smile took over her face.

'How lovely, Jenny, breakfast in bed! No one has done that for me since Peter died, and it was one of my favourite things.'

'You deserve it for putting up with me and my neglect of you.'

'Rubbish, girl. You're quite entitled to your friendships. And you've got all this business to sort out.'

'That might remain as a mystery at the rate we're going.'

'Well, give it your best shot for the sake of Gloria Standish.'

'I'll try. She does want to know the truth.'

Aunt Judy pulled the pillows behind her and I placed the tray on her lap, passing her the napkin. She caught my hand in hers. 'Thank you, Jenny. I'm sorry about what I said to that reporter fellow. I think I was jealous.'

'What do you mean?'

'When he said you were Gloria's adopted daughter. I thought you had agreed to it, you see, and I always think of you as the daughter I never had.'

I looked at her in amazement. 'Do you? Well, in that case I have been a most neglectful daughter and must make you breakfast in bed more often.'

'You don't mind? I thought you might think I was too presumptive.'

I sat on the edge of the bed and looked straight at her. 'Aunt Judy, since my mother died – no, before that, when she stopped knowing who I was – I have longed to have a mother again. Not any mother, but family. I think you will do very nicely!'

My aunt returned to her normal, practical self. 'Well, in that case, would you kindly fetch the salt? You know perfectly well I can't eat a boiled egg without salt.'

I fetched it for her, and while I watched her sprinkle it into her egg, the phone rang. I tried to walk sedately down the stairs but excitement made me hurry, and I grabbed it off its cradle. I answered with the number and was rewarded by hearing Jim say, 'Hello, darling Jen, how are you today?'

I wished I had closed my aunt's bedroom door. 'I'm fine, Jim. How are you?'

It sounded so formal. But he realised what was happening. 'I guess your aunt is within earshot.'

'Yes.'

'She knows we are together, Jenny, so I wouldn't worry about her hearing. What are you doing today? Visiting Gloria, I expect.'

Half my mind was savouring the phrase, 'we are together,' but I answered, 'Yes, I shall go this morning and check she's okay. Is it today that Freddie comes back from Germany?'

'I believe so, which is good because you can't be checking on her every day for the rest of her life.'

'Perhaps not. I wanted to ask you a few things yesterday, but other matters sort of took over. Can we meet up?'

'I think Aunt Gloria would like to see her nephew, wouldn't she?'

'Good thought. I plan on being there at about ten-thirty. I think they'll let me in this morning rather than during visiting hours, unless Freddie beats me to it.'

'Meanwhile, you have a nice breakfast with your lovely perceptive aunt.'

'Too late. I've had mine and taken up hers.'

'You took her breakfast in bed?'

'Yes, why?'

'Nothing. I was only thinking you'd make someone a wonderful wife.'

I didn't know what to say, so I kept quiet.

'Jenny, I haven't offended you, have I?'

'No, of course not. I'll see you later. Bye for now, Jim.'

'Bye, darling. See you soon.'

As I put down the phone, I realised I had twiddled the lead into a mass of untidy swirls. I began to sort it out, smiling as I replayed the conversation in my mind. What had he meant by saying I'd make someone a wonderful wife? Was it a proposal? I thought of Jim in his house with Stephen. Perhaps he had called him for breakfast now... Would I be able to cope with his disabled son? A doubt crept unwanted into my mind. Suppose Jim was looking for a woman merely to help look after Stephen? Why else would he be interested in a recluse like me?

By the time Aunt Judy came downstairs, I had decided that from now on I would have to keep things firmly on a business footing, however I felt. I would explain it to Aunt Judy, so that I kept my resolve. And as for moving from London, well, I was better as far away from Jim as I could be.

But I felt so sad and disappointed that I could hardly speak to my aunt for my tears.

'Jenny, what is it? Has something happened?'

I shook my head – how could I tell her that I was scared Jim had an ulterior motive? She liked him; that was clear. I went upstairs to wash my face and try to think things through.

34

I still couldn't speak to Aunt Judy about how I felt when I came back downstairs. From wanting desperately to see Jim, I now felt as if I wanted to avoid him. What was the matter with me? Was this just my own thinking, or was he really looking for help with Stephen?

'You will have to tell me what the matter is, Jenny. Something to do with Jim, I suppose?'

He was right about her being perceptive. I didn't say anything. Aunt Judy continued. 'You know, my dear, it is really hard when love comes late. My friend met someone who was your age. She had been married briefly before but he had died in the war, so she had all that grief to tackle as well. Anyway, this chap was an absolute charmer and she was really unsure. She went off to Spain for the winter and missed him so badly that she came back immediately after Christmas.'

'Was he pleased to see her?'

'Extremely pleased. He thought he had lost her and had been drooping around visiting all her friends trying to find out how she was. He was quite a pathetic soul without her.'

'So what happened?'

'Nearly a fairy tale ending. I say "nearly" because they were both rather used to being on their own, so for about two years they lived separately. Then she became very ill with cancer and she wanted to marry him before she died, so they got married and he moved in and cared for her. '

'Did she die?'

'Not then. She went into remission and they had a great time – that must have lasted about eighteen months, I should think, but the cancer returned. He was there beside her while she went through the whole wretched chemo treatment again. He thought she was wonderful throughout. He was heartbroken when she died.'

'I know so little about relationships, Aunt Judy.'

'You only find out as you go along! It's like learning to swim. You have to take your feet off the ground to learn how.'

'But I might be a really poor judge of character and end up getting into hot water!'

We both started to laugh at the mix of metaphors.

'I think Jim is quite an honest man; do you have a problem with him?'

'He has a son who has a disability – well, nephew, really – who he looks after.'

'I see. So you're worried about becoming a carer?'

'I'm worried that might be the only reason he likes me. He knows I cared for Mother and Father.'

'I think two caring people recognise the value of that in each other. If the boy has been Jim's responsibility for many years, then he has proved he is willing to accept that responsibility.'

'Stephen's a young man now.' As I thought about Stephen I remembered that Jim said he was working towards independent living.

'You know, Aunt Judy, I've just remembered that Jim thinks he will soon be moving out. Now I feel really guilty that I have doubted Jim at all.'

'You know, dear, if Stephen does need care, you will be able to cope. You are far more adaptable than you think.'

But I was feeling deeply ashamed that I had not had the generosity of spirit to willingly accept any of the responsibilities that came with Jim. As I stood there, I shot up a silent prayer that God would show me. Even as I prayed, I recognised it was nonsense to think that Jim only liked me because I might make a carer for Stephen. The bubble of excitement started to fill me again.

'I'd better go and see Gloria. Jim will be there; is it okay for him to come back?'

'Of course, dear. And give Gloria my best regards, if she remembers a little brat from the days when she helped us work for Brownie badges!'

I grabbed my coat and then gave her a quick hug before walking out serenely to the car, my mind full of the prospect of meeting Jim.

I arrived before Jim. Gloria was pacing around the ward fully clothed, and we were both shown into the visitors' area.

'I'm afraid not even honorary daughters are allowed on the ward while the doctor is doing his rounds,' I was told by the Sister. The word 'honorary' was not lost on me. Somewhere along the line I had been rumbled as not a true adopted daughter.

'Won't you miss out on seeing the doctor?' I asked Gloria as we tried to make ourselves comfortable in the old hospital chairs.

'I'm going home. I would have gone yesterday but they insisted someone should be with me.'

'Have you found someone?'

'I've told them Mrs D who does cleaning for me will be there when they take me back and must listen to all instructions.'

'But she doesn't stay overnight, does she?'

'No, and I don't want her to.'

I didn't like this; it seemed to be leading up to an involvement I was not ready for.

'Will Freddie be back today?'

'Yes. But if he has his shrew of a wife with him, then I don't want them staying.'

I let that one go. Gloria must have some reason for disliking her daughter-in-law, but it was none of my business.

'What about one of your friends?'

'Can't think of anyone. I thought you might stay.'

'I don't think I can. I'm here to visit my aunt. I could look in on you tomorrow morning, but I do have to get back to London in the next couple of days.'

Gloria looked at me. She had obviously not expected me to refuse. 'I thought we had things to talk about. Are you still investigating what happened?'

I was worried someone else would hear us. Probably I was being paranoid, but Graham had spooked me.

'Don't you go worrying about anything. We'll have plenty of time to talk, I'm sure.'

'You haven't answered my question.'

Sister looked round the corner where we were sitting. 'Mrs Standish, the doctor would like a word with you before you go with your daughter. So can you hang on for a while?'

'Not too long, I hope. Jenny has other things to do.'

'I'm sure she has time to wait a bit.'

'Yes, that's fine,' I said. I was wondering what had happened to Jim.

'Gloria, you haven't had a message from Jim, have you?'

'No. Should he have left a message?'

'I said I'd see him here. He knows I'm visiting you so he was going to come as well.'

'Is he the one who says he's my nephew?'

I nodded.

'Oh dear, I think I gave the game away. One of the nurses was asking after my family and I told her I was an only child.'

'It can't be that – he could have been Henry's nephew.'

'She asked if Henry had brothers and sisters and I said "no." It was only then that I remembered Jim had said he was my nephew. But I didn't think it mattered because he wouldn't come here again.'

'I'll ask on the desk if he's been here. I'll tell them that you like him being your nephew. They should understand that; after all, you decided I was your daughter.'

'Go then, dear, before Jim gets arrested.'

I went up to the desk. There was no one around, but I could see a group of people around one of the beds, and Sister was among them. I hovered at the desk, not wanting to intrude on another patient's information. Eventually she spotted me and came over.

'Did my friend Jim come to see Gloria? The man she calls her nephew?'

'The porters sent him away. He's no relative of Gloria's.'

'I know, but nor am I. She sometimes calls her younger friends "nephews" or "nieces". As you know, she refers to me as her daughter, but I'm really only a friend.'

'Oh, I see. We thought he had some sort of hold over her, some claim on her inheritance.'

'Nothing like that. Nor have I, for that matter. We became concerned about her. I live in north London, so I drove up to see her. It's as well I did, really.'

'I'll make a phone call or two and see if I can discover the whereabouts of your friend. I'd better finish the round with the doctor first.'

I reported back to Gloria. She was becoming a little upset, but there was nothing we could do. I tried to distract her. 'Did Freddie say when he was coming?'

'He said around lunchtime, so I told him I'd probably be home by then so he'd better go there. I thought you'd be able to take me. At least, that's what I told the nurse. I might have been in a bit of a pickle if you hadn't turned up.'

'I daresay they'd have rung to see where I was! I did leave my aunt's phone number at the desk the other day. But I thought someone from the hospital was taking you home?'

'Oh no, dear. They'll tell you what I need and everything.'

I wondered whether Gloria was thinking straight, but I let it go because I was finding it difficult to keep calm. I kept glancing at the door and then at the slowly moving group of doctors and nurses as they worked their way round from bed to bed. What could have happened to Jim? So much for keeping out of the limelight; our link with Gloria was becoming more public by the minute.

'I'm going to make you a cup of tea, Gloria, and then if you think you'll be all right, I shall pop down to the porters' desk and see if they know what happened to Jim, then both our minds can be put at rest. I think Sister is going to be a long time this morning so I don't really want to wait for her.'

'That's a good idea, Jenny.'

She seemed to have shrunk a little. The spark I had so admired in her seemed to have gone. Maybe she was becoming a little confused; I hoped not.

'If Sister comes over, tell her I'll be back quickly. I know you want me here when the doctor sees you, but he has at least three or four patients to talk to yet.'

Gloria nodded. I thought I had better not take too long.

It was easy to find the porters' desk. It was near the entrance and surrounded by taxi drivers who obviously used it as a named meeting point. Summoning all my courage, I moved past them up to the desk. There was a porter on the phone. I waited patiently while he finished the call.

'Hello, I'm looking for a visitor called Jim Tyler. He wanted to visit our friend Gloria this morning, but was not allowed to see her. Do you know what happened to him?'

'I do. What has it got to do with you?'

'I arranged to meet him when we visited Gloria, and now I don't know where he is.'

'And who are you, did you say?'

'I'm Jenny Drake. A friend of Gloria Standish, although she does sometimes call me her adopted daughter.'

'Why's that, then?'

'Perhaps she always wanted a daughter? To her, I'm a daughter, and my friend Jim is a nephew.'

'I wonder if you'd sit over there for a minute. I'll make a call or two.'

I worried as I sat on a brown vinyl seat in the waiting area. Gloria was on her own and the doctor would be talking to her. I watched the clock over the porters' desk. Ten minutes had passed. The porter seemed to be making a lot of calls; I wondered if he had forgotten about me.

'Excuse me, I'd better get back to Gloria for a minute; the doctor is going to talk to her and she wanted me there. She's on Ward C2. Would you be able to leave a message up there?'

'Look, I'm trying to sort this out for you here. I can't be ringing up to wards.'

'Thank you very much for all you're doing. But I'd better go back to be with Gloria and come back again as soon as I have spoken to the doctor.'

I didn't give him time to protest but made my way quickly up to the ward, where I found Gloria encircled by the doctor and nurses.

'Ah, here she is,' said the Sister.

'Sorry, I was trying to find out what had happened to my friend.'

The doctor turned to me. 'Your mother would like to be discharged. I am happy with that as long as there is someone who will stay with her.'

'Her son comes home any minute now. He has been abroad.'

'Won't you be able to stay with her?'

Gloria was looking at me pleadingly.

'I am not sure I will be able to, but if Freddie can't then I'll see what I can do.'

'Thank you, Jenny, thank you,' said Gloria, then she turned her attention to her assembled audience. 'Now you see why she's my adopted daughter!'

I sincerely hoped Freddie would be home safe and sound and installed in Gloria's farmhouse. Meanwhile, where was Jim?

35

I stopped at the porters' desk on the way out of the hospital with Gloria, much to the annoyance of the porter wheeling the hospital chair she had been given. The same chap I had spoken to before was apologetic in an off-hand kind of way. 'I can't find out what happened to him. Someone said he was escorted off the premises, but that might have been someone else. Does he have a beard?'

'No, he doesn't.'

'Well, this chap did. So I don't know what happened to your Mr Tyler.'

If he didn't know, then I had no idea who would. Perhaps once I'd taken Gloria home I could ring around to see if I could find him. The porter had moved close to the automatic doors and Gloria had no coat on, so I hurried to get her into the warmer confines of my car as soon as possible.

Gloria sat in the passenger seat beside me and talked all the way as I drove her home. There was no sign of the cough that I had heard during the week, and she seemed in fine spirits.

'Your cough has cleared up quickly,' I said.

'Cough? Oh, that comes and goes.' There was something odd about the way she said it. I wondered why she had a cough that came and went. I couldn't look at her to see if her face gave her away; it was pouring with rain and I needed to keep my eyes on the road.

'Gloria, this may sound like a silly question, but how bad was your cough? Do you think it was your chest that made you too ill to move so that you nearly froze to death?'

'Don't exaggerate, dear. I didn't nearly freeze to death. I only got a bit cold. That's all.'

I waited until I had gone round a series of hilly bends before I spoke again. 'Gloria, you were nearly gone. You had hypothermia. You told me the doctor said it was a good job we arrived when we did, because you probably wouldn't have made it.'

'I don't think it was the cough that did that.'

I was remembering what Graham had said. Had Gloria been drugged? 'Did anybody come to see you that day, the day we found you?'

'I can't remember. I know Mrs D wasn't in – she was on holiday. She usually makes me a hot dinner, too. It was a day or two before you arrived, I think. Somebody came about my front wall. Said he'd hit it with his car when he came round the corner. I couldn't think what corner, but he drew me a diagram. Gave me his insurance details. I thought that was good of him, so I gave him a cup of tea. Nice man.'

My spine was tingling with fear. I kept my eyes on the road. We were nearly there. As calmly as possible I said, 'Oh, we'll have to have a look when we get back. And if you give me the details, I'll see what's happening about a repair.'

'That's kind of you, dear. You're a wonderful daughter.'

'We can stop pretending now, Gloria! Let's see if your son is in.'

There was no sign of Freddie or of Jim. I looked at Gloria's phone to see if she had an answering machine; she didn't. The place was very cold and felt damp. I wrapped Gloria up in front of the dead fire and boiled a kettle for a hot-water bottle for her so that she wouldn't get too cold while I warmed the place up. I couldn't see the little heater we had used on the night we found Gloria. I guessed Mary Davies had put it back in its usual place.

'Where's your electric fan heater, Gloria?'

'I usually have that on in the kitchen.'

I checked but couldn't see it. There was enough kindling and old newspaper in a bucket by the log basket, but no logs, so I went out via the kitchen door to find some. Outdoors felt huge and menacing, and I steeled myself to reach the woodpile, then raced back in with only three small logs and bolted the door behind me. I would have to take the basket with me next time and force myself to stay long enough to bring in a good supply. I realised this was the first near panic attack I'd had outside for a while.

When I went back into the sitting room, the cosily wrapped Gloria was staring at her mantelpiece. 'Could you straighten that photo, dear, and move the vase along a bit. I don't know what Mrs D's been doing, but everything looks a bit different.'

I sorted out her mantelpiece for her. Then it was the coffee table and the bookshelves. In Gloria's eyes everything needed to be put straight, although to me it looked fine. I stopped rearranging everything to her satisfaction and told her I must light the fire.

The logs were damp and sizzled for a few minutes before sending up smoke and losing any glow. I reset the fire, using more newspaper; some of it wound up into knots as I was running out of kindling. I sat there blowing at the tiny red flame.

'Use those bellows, dear. I always do,' said Gloria. It occurred to me that if I hadn't dashed in and immediately made her an invalid by wrapping her up in the patchwork cover, she would probably have lit the fire with no trouble at all. But the bellows puffed the small flame into something that would catch.

Eventually, I had lit the fire and could safely leave Gloria for a bit to phone around to try to find Jim. There was no response from his house phone. I rang my aunt to see if he'd left a message there, but he hadn't. I nearly forgot to tell her that I was with Gloria because her son, Freddie, hadn't yet arrived.

I made a cup of tea for us both, and it was only as I brought it back to the front room that I realised I had forgotten all about the mysterious visitor who'd said he had hit the front wall of her property. I presumed that would be by the farm gate. I didn't trust myself to walk down the track without panicking. I could look at the diagram, though.

'Where's that picture about the wall?' I asked Gloria.

She pointed at her handbag. 'I expect I tucked it in there, dear. I usually do if there's something I mustn't lose.'

The bag was full of letters and notes to herself. But there was one very neatly folded piece of green paper with a diagram on it.

'Is this it?'

'Yes – open it up and you'll see where he said he hit the wall.'

When I unfolded the paper I saw a very accurate, neat drawing of the farm gate and the walls either side. There was a cross on the wall nearest to the side the gate opened. Against it was written, 'Dent to brickwork. Possible damage to three bricks.' There was something very familiar about the writing.

'How old was this man, Gloria? Any idea?'

'Much, much older than you. Older than Jim, too. Probably mid-seventies?'

My breathing went haywire. I tried to take control of myself without upsetting Gloria. So much for the theory that any of the researchers would be too old by now to be harmful. I looked again to check. Yes, the writing looked as if it could be the same as in the records of the drug trials which were stored in Henry's box file.

I realised everything was not quite in place in this room because, most probably, it had been searched. Perhaps to retrieve this drawing, which I had unwittingly taken into the hospital when I had picked up Gloria's bag instead of mine.

So were we in immediate danger? If so, who could help us now? Gloria was telling me about the photos on the mantelpiece, who was in them and where they had been taken. I couldn't listen; I needed space to think.

'I'll find us some lunch, Gloria. I'm really hungry.'

I went through to the cold kitchen and found eggs and some rather stale bread. While I cooked scrambled egg on toast I tried to run all the different scenarios and my suspicions through my mind. Who could help me find Jim, and how could I keep myself and Gloria safe?

The eggs stuck to the bottom of the pan while I went round and checked that every door was locked and bolted. By the time I had done that, I had decided I would have to ring Graham, the pretend journalist. He was our only hope.

But was he able to help us, or was he working with the mysterious visitor whose writing was so much like that of the researcher who had signed himself 'C. W.' in the pharmaceutical company records?

36

I was standing by the phone, clenching my fists so hard that I could feel my nails in my palms. I tried to relax myself and think whether there was any way I could find Jim on my own. With no one here to look after Gloria, I was reluctant to go off anywhere to hunt for him. Anyway, where would I go? I had drawn a blank at the hospital. I had no choice but to contact Graham.

I rang the number from his private investigator card. There was no reply; the ringing went to an answerphone. I was ready for this, having decided that I had better leave a message as if I didn't know him.

'Oh, hello. I wonder if you can help me. A friend of mine seems to have disappeared and although he hasn't been gone long, I am rather concerned because it's unlike him not to contact me. My phone number is...' and I gave Gloria's number. 'Thank you.'

After leaving the message, I stood there worrying that I shouldn't have given Gloria's number. I wasn't sure if Graham would recognise my voice. I needn't have been anxious about that: the phone rang while I was standing there. 'Hello, is that you, Miss Drake? Who's gone missing? Or was that simply for the answerphone?'

'It's Jim.' I was trembling as I outlined what had happened at the hospital. 'And in fact her son, Freddie, should be here by now too. But I don't know what flight he was on.'

'I can help you with that. The incoming flights from Germany have been delayed. Problem with air control somewhere. Jim's disappearance is a bit odd, though.'

'There are other things, but it might be good if you were to come here to discuss them.'

'I'll be right over. How's Mrs Standish?'

'Remarkably good.'

'I'll be with you within half an hour.'

When I hung up, Gloria was calling me. I went and helped her upstairs to go to her bathroom. It made me realise that she wasn't ready to be left on her own.

After I returned her to her seat by the fire, I made my next dash to the woodpile, this time managing to half-fill the log basket. I wouldn't have been able to carry more. I made up the fire which looked about to go out, and then, with Gloria's permission, I rang Mary Davies.

'Hello, Mrs Davies. Jenny here, friend of Gloria.'

'Hello.'

'Gloria's home.'

'That's good. She's better, is she?'

I realised that Mary Davies knew nothing about looking after her when she was home. 'Gloria seems to think you are coming round to look after her. Has she got that wrong?'

'First I've heard about it. I'm all tied up today with my grandson. Sorry.'

'Are you sure you couldn't pop over for a bit? I've been here since I brought her back from hospital.'

'No, sorry, he's here now. He's not well, you see, so he's not at school.'

'Would you be able to pop over tomorrow, do you think?'

'I could do some cleaning for her tomorrow. I took the liberty of not coming in today as she was in hospital.'

'Would you be able to come all day if Freddie's not here? To keep her company and maybe make her tea as well?'

'I'd have to be home by five-thirty.'

I had to settle for that. I thought I would contact Gloria's family doctor later and explain that she was on her own. I went back to Gloria and told her about the phone call. 'Why didn't she know you were coming home? I thought you rang her?'

'I meant to ring her,' said Gloria. 'But it doesn't matter: you're here today.'

'Well, I'm not too pleased,' was all I managed to say. I tried to put to one side that Gloria seemed to have tricked me into bringing her back to an empty house. My mind was really working overtime about the fact that Mary Davies hadn't cleaned at all. Someone else had definitely been here, then. I was not paranoid.

There was a knock on the door. I forced myself to go to open it. Although I was expecting Graham to come, I was fearful that it might be someone else.

To my amazement and joy it was Jim, wearing a dark brown coat with a hood, like Graham's. He took me in his arms and gave me a great bear hug. I didn't know whether to be cross with him or hug him back. But I was so pleased to see him that I clung to him. Together, we walked back into the front room. 'Gloria, it's Jim.'

'Well, thank goodness you've turned up. Where have you been? Your lady has been worrying herself sick about you. She thought you'd been arrested.'

'Not quite. I was taken to the police station for questioning, though. Graham came and talked to them and they let me go. Graham took me back to his house for us to find out where you were, and you rang while I was there.'

'Why didn't he say?' Even as I asked I realised that Graham was probably concerned that his phone was bugged, as we had been at Jim's house. Something occurred to me and I quickly grabbed a pen and paper. I wrote, *Someone unknown has been in Gloria's house. Do you think it's bugged?*

Jim read it and raised his eyebrows.

'What's going on?' asked Gloria. We both turned to her with our fingers up to our lips.

'Excuse me,' she said. 'Perhaps you two lovebirds had better stop that and fetch some more wood for the fire.'

'Sorry, Gloria,' said Jim. 'It's been a very difficult day, and I'm so glad to find Jenny here safely with you. Although you caused some of it, you know, chatting to the nurses so that they twigged I wasn't your nephew. I went up to the desk and said I was, so they called the porters!'

All credit to Gloria – she was able to come up with a retort. 'I can call my friends what I want. You two are like relations when I need them. What would I have done without you?'

'Well, I forgive you. I know you didn't mean any harm.' He picked up the log basket. 'Where am I going with this, Jenny?'

'I'll show you.'

At the front door, I filled him in with all that had happened. I outlined my suspicions that the man who had reported hitting the wall was probably the same person who had been in the house. He may have been trying to find his diagram to avoid being implicated in this whole business. Then I quickly told him that I was expecting Graham any minute, that Freddie was probably delayed and that Mary Davies couldn't come to sleep overnight.

'OK, well, we can't be out here too long. Graham isn't coming yet, that's why I was wearing his coat, we think his house is being watched. Freddie and his wife are at Graham's house. Freddie will come later but someone will need to go to "collect" him from the airport. So it doesn't matter that you can't sleep here tonight, as they will.'

'But what about the chap who hit the wall? His writing was very like that researcher's on the data collection forms.'

'It could well be him. Graham has found out that security was in a mess at the company. A new security officer came in and found discrepancies. They were being followed up by Dan, the first person to "commit suicide". We think he had confronted our man and told him he would be exposed.'

'Let's walk to look at the wall. Gloria and I have discussed it, so that won't look strange.'

Walking down the farm track was not too bad with my arm tucked into Jim's. He examined the wall carefully.

'Something might have hit it, but I don't see any reason to report it to the owner.'

'I think we ought to get back to Gloria. She's been on her own for quite a time.'

'Wait a minute. Let's just pray for everyone's safety.' Jim bowed his head. 'Lord, we need you here. Keep us safe tonight and do a great work in protecting us, and especially Gloria. Amen.'

We smiled at each other. I felt calmer.

Carrying the heavy basket of logs between us, we heaved it back into the house. Jim took it from me to place it in the hearth. As I turned back to Gloria, I realised she was trembling. 'What's the matter, Gloria?'

'I'm not feeling so good, dear. Come and put that blanket back round me, would you?' I picked up the patchwork cover, and as I bent over to tuck it around her, she whispered in my ear, 'I think there's someone in the kitchen.' In turn, I mouthed it to Jim, who picked up the poker and crept towards the door.

I tried to keep up ordinary chatter with Gloria. 'We looked at the wall while we were outside. I think maybe someone has damaged it a bit. It was good of him to own up about it, though. Perhaps your mysterious gentleman is one of those rare things – a true gent.'

'Not many of those around these days.' Gloria's eyes were darting about. She looked terrified. I took her hand. There was nothing we could do. I was praying that Jim would be all right.

He called from the kitchen, 'Who'd like tea? Gloria, do you have any coffee?'

I wondered if it was a trap. Could someone be forcing him to shout this?

I looked at Gloria; she couldn't say anything. 'Tea for both of us I think, Jim. Thanks. If you want coffee, it's in the top cupboard over the kettle.'

We hardly moved; I was expecting someone to bring Jim in at gunpoint. Nothing happened like that. Jim carried the hot drinks through.

'No one there,' he mouthed at Gloria, who let out a long breath. My pounding heart seemed to slow a little, but he turned to me and said, 'I thought it best to lock up. It's getting a bit dark.'

I knew I had locked and bolted that door earlier. We had gone out of the front door to look at the wall and collect logs. No one had unbolted it. No one should have been in that kitchen.

37

We drank our tea in an uneasy silence, broken only by Jim and myself offering a few comments about the weather, the lovely colour in Gloria's patchwork blanket and the fact that I had always wanted a cat. To me, the tea tasted like dishwater, and the minutes hung back, heavy laden.

I couldn't keep my mind in the present. For a moment I was on a beach, watching someone trying to fly. Then I was noticing the back of Jim's head in the mirror in my front room. Thinking of my house gave me an enormous longing to be in my own home, where all was neat and tidy and full of my mother's favourite furniture. I wanted to smell the beeswax while I was polishing, and to see the pile of scones when I had finished baking. I wished I had some now to share around and perhaps relax the atmosphere. I worried that nothing else would feel like home for me. I would have to discuss that with Jim, whose hand was now holding mine.

I told Gloria that if Freddie didn't come, then either Jim or I would stay the night. She looked terrified but managed to say, 'You could both stay if you want. I don't mind about sleeping arrangements.'

This broke our collective nervousness. I blushed. Jim laughed, 'No need for us both to stay; we're not quite inseparable yet!'

I wasn't sure I agreed with him. The thought of home was a really strong pull, though. Or was it the normality I craved? I was fed up with feeling nervous, although, of course, I had been experiencing that for about fifty years. But this was a real fear; I could feel it prickle through me.

We sat there, expectant, not knowing what would happen or when.

'Shall we see what's on the television?' said Jim. 'We all seem too tired to talk.' He stood up to move towards the corner where the television was.

There was a sudden noise outside.

I jumped up, knocking over the table with the tray. Gloria was clutching the arms of her chair as if she would never let go. Jim was immediately between us, pulling me down beside him, with his body shielding Gloria.

'It's all right. Graham's outside with the police. Keep still.'

A man shot through the house, right past the back of Jim and out through the other door from the sitting room. Two policemen were following. We heard the front door open and someone fall down. Then quiet. Voices were starting outside.

Jim stood up as Graham walked in. 'All over, ladies. Sorry I couldn't warn you. It's done: they've got him.'

Gloria got out of her chair and shuffled over to the window, losing her blanket as she went. I scooped it into her chair, conscious of the fire being so close. Jim's arms went round my shoulders. 'Are you all right, Jen darling?'

I collapsed into a blubbering mess. I cried as I leant against Jim's strong body. I couldn't quite piece it all together, but the relief that we were all safe simply overwhelmed me. He carefully led me over to the settee and sat next to me.

'Don't know what's the matter with you, girl,' said Gloria, who was peering out of the window. 'They've got him. He's the chap who told me he'd hit my wall.'

From where I sat I could see the police leading someone away. 'Freddie?' I asked, in total incomprehension.

'That's not my Freddie,' said Gloria. 'I knew something fishy was going on as soon as you said he ate your scones. Freddie hates the things. That's when I spoke to Graham here.'

'So Gloria, you've been in on this from the start?'

'I've been in on this since Henry died. I was sure it wasn't suicide. But I had to prove it.'

'I think we've proved it now,' said Graham. 'We have wonderful footage of him telling you about the wall and then coming to try to find his diagram. I'm only sorry we didn't get him on camera spiking your drink.'

Gloria's voice had a slight tremble as she spoke, 'I could've died, you know.'

'Probably not,' said Graham. 'I tried to ring you earlier that day, but when there was no answer I came over to check on you. I was right behind these two on the road when they found you.'

'Didn't I say we were being followed, Jim?'

'Yes, you did. And I thought you were being nervous. I'm sorry.'

'I'd seen the box file already, I'm afraid,' said Graham. 'But we had to get you both here somehow.'

'Why?' I asked.

'One reason was to pool information, but also because our suspect was getting too close to finding out it was me who was investigating Henry's death. I needed a diversion, and then when Jim asked about Henry at the library, I was pretty sure he wouldn't take a lot of notice of amateurs like you, especially if I tipped Jim off.'

'So you knew?' I was looking at Jim in astonishment. How had he deceived me?

Jim looked uncomfortable. 'Not before that day when Graham came round. He tried to tell you, but you were so nervous he thought it was better if you didn't know everything. He did alert you to the fact that he was a private investigator, though, so you did exactly right to ring him when you needed to, without giving anything away.'

'So who was the chap who pretended to be Freddie and ate my scones?'

'Colin Windrush. A researcher at Phoenix Pharmaceuticals. He was stealing drugs to sell; the experimental ones plus others. Dan Wallis was going to expose him.'

I shrugged. I was too tired to think about it all. I wanted to get back to something familiar. I asked Jim, 'So is all this cloak-and-dagger stuff finally over, then?'

'Yes. Completely.'

'Well, in that case, if I'm not needed here, I'd better get back to Aunt Judy and pack up to go home.'

'You're not going, are you?' Jim looked horrified.

'I think I need to. I have an appointment with Mike Lewis, for one thing.'

'Surely it would be better to ring him and spend a little time making it up to your aunt? Anyway, the police might want to talk to you.' There was a tone of desperation in his voice.

My anxiety began to resurface. 'I thought it was all over.'

'Well, sort of. Please stay in Devon a little while longer. Not for the mystery, but for us.'

I looked at Jim, unsure how to respond.

Gloria broke the silence. 'I think you'd better, Jenny. You and Jim have a few things to sort out. In fact, as your adoptive mother, I order you to do something normal with Jim, now you're not involved in this sleuthing.' She broke off, coughing.

Normal with Jim. The phrase went round my mind as I began to imagine a new normality. My heart was telling me to stay. Here I was safe with Jim. I needed a few days to get over the trauma of our adventures. I leaned back against Jim's warmth. His arms encircled me.

'Okay, Gloria. I'll stay, but on one condition.'

'What's that?' She looked quite worried about what I would say.

'You stop calling me your adopted daughter. Aunt Judy is jealous.'

'I must renew my acquaintance with this Aunt Judy of yours. She sounds like someone I would get on with very well.'

'Only allow that, Jen, if they promise not to fight over who is the mother of my good lady,' said Jim.

I smiled. The knowledge that a wonderful man wanted to call me his good lady was comforting and exciting all at once. I didn't know what the future held. But I felt more grounded than I had for decades. Perhaps we would be together forever. I silently prayed that this might be so, sure in the knowledge that Jim would have already done so.

Epilogue

I expected to stay on in Devon for another week or so, but somehow that stretched to more than three. So it was a full four weeks before I was back in the Psychology Department for my much-postponed appointment with Mike Lewis. There was no one in the waiting area when I arrived, but I was pleased when Mike called me in a little early, because by then a couple had turned up with three loud children clamouring for their parents' attention, completely destroying my attempts to mentally order what I wanted to say in the session.

Mike's room was an oasis of quiet, albeit with less than perfect surroundings. There were no dirty mugs to be seen, but it looked as if he was halfway through sorting out his filing cabinet, and there were no fewer than four piles of files on his desk, jammed up against each other as if their closeness would make the room seem tidy. The sad plant had been pushed into a corner on the windowsill, dust covering its leaves.

I sat on the chair by the door, impatient for Mike to stop shuffling about on his desk and to be ready to hear all my news. He finally found my file from the third leaning pile and turned to give me his full attention.

I waited for his usual opening line: 'How was your journey here, Jenny?'

'Very pleasant. A breezy but invigorating walk to the station and an easy ride on the Tube. When I was walking from the station to here I was surprised to see they're still working on the road outside your department. Whatever are they doing to take so long to finish?'

Mike sat there looking at me as if I were an alien, then pulled himself into professional mode. 'No feelings of panic? No problems?'

'Not one. I've done this journey so many times that it was easy.' I couldn't keep a note of triumph out of my voice. Before he could say anything, I explained that the extra time I had staying with my aunt had been so relaxing that I had begun to make real progress.

'With or without the help of your friend?' asked Dr Lewis.

'Mostly with Jim, at first. But I have been trying a few things out myself.'

'So solving your mystery has freed you up?'

'I'm not sure about that. I was quite wobbly for a few days, although maybe that was to be expected. I had to give a statement to the police, too. That was exhausting. I wasn't ready to come home immediately.'

'But obviously you've now been able to do it somehow. How did you manage the drive back to London? Did Jim come with you?'

'No, he needed to stay in Devon. I coped, driving myself; mostly by remembering I had done it before and could do it again.'

Mike smiled and stroked his beard. I thought it must be very satisfying to have a stuck client like me make such huge progress.

'Okay, well it's obvious that you've made a massive step forward, which we can build on. But first, you'll have to tell me all about how the mystery unfolded, how everything is for you now, and what the future holds.'

I laughed and Mike joined in. This whole session was feeling so different.

I began telling him all about the day I took Gloria home from the hospital. That was a truly difficult afternoon. I told him how frightened I was, especially when it became clear that Gloria's visitor, the man who had said he'd damaged her wall, may well have been the same person who had stolen the hallucinogenic drugs.

'I nearly lost it when we thought someone was in the kitchen and the back door of her cottage was unlocked. Jim has told me since that when he went out to the kitchen, he was pretty sure that the coat on the back of the door was moving as if the door had just been closed as someone left. He locked it immediately. He had already alerted the police that the suspect might be there, so he knew they were on the way.'

'Who did Jim think had been in the kitchen?'

'Colin Windrush. And he was right. Windrush used to be a researcher at Phoenix Pharmaceuticals, back in 1956, and had been stealthily removing drugs to sell. When he was nearly exposed by Dan Wallis, he slipped one of the stolen tablets into his drink. He did exactly the same to Henry Standish.'

'I see; so where does Freddie come into all of this?'

'He doesn't. It wasn't Freddie who had come to see me; it was Colin Windrush posing as Freddie. He didn't know Freddie hated scones, so when I spoke to Gloria she knew instantly that it wasn't him, so she contacted Jim and Graham Clark, the private detective.'

'Do you think this Windrush chap wanted to poison you, too?'

'Maybe. I'll never know. But I threw the tea and scones away because even though I thought he was Freddie, I was suspicious of him.'

'Did he drug Gloria?'

'That's very likely, although he was more subtle about it. Gloria didn't tell us at the time, but the doctors told her off for taking too many cold relief tablets – "A dangerously high dose". But she hadn't taken anything apart from some honey and lemon linctus. She did have bronchitis, though, with her coughing slightly exaggerated for my benefit, I suspect. And they found the shadow on her lungs, of course.'

'Yes, I am sorry. How is she?'

'Her usual feisty self! The prognosis is still poor, but she says she doesn't care if she goes to her Maker now. She is satisfied to have proved Henry didn't commit suicide. She's loving every day of her life, filling it with friends she invites round. Her house is full of laughter, and her new full-time carer spends most of the time making tea.'

'It must be a real relief to Gloria, to know the truth about Henry. But, you've had a tremendously exciting time and emerged triumphant too! What about you and your friend, what's happening there?'

I could feel the heat rise up my body and cover my face. Mike continued to look at me, his head slightly to one side, waiting expectantly.

'We've been seeing a lot of each other and he wants me to move to Devon.'

'And do you plan to do that?'

'So far I've told him I couldn't possibly. But...'

I closed my eyes. I remembered stubby hands in the café, an arm round my shoulder as we sat by a crackling fire. His wish to call me 'darling'. His idea of us together. The recent outings we'd had with Stephen. How comfortable I felt with him when he prayed. But most of all, my feelings were almost shouting, *I miss him. I can't be without him. I want to see him.*

'I thought I wanted to be back in London. I was desperate to be in my own home. To have my own things around me, to be able to lock my own front door. Now, well...' I paused. I wasn't sure whether I was ready to tell anyone how I felt, although I knew I would have to tell Jim soon. Mike waited for my next words. I wasn't panicking but my heart was racing. I told him, 'Nothing seems right. It's my parents' house, not mine. Even though I can now walk in the garden, visit my neighbours and easily manage coming to see you, I feel as if I am in the wrong place.'

Mike nodded slowly. His question came gently. 'And where is the right place, Jenny?'

I hardly paused before saying with conviction, 'With Jim. Definitely. I've decided to move to Devon, staying with my aunt for now while I sort things out. Jim has asked me to marry him, and I'm ashamed to say that the main thing that has stopped me saying "yes" is the fact that I couldn't even think about leaving London.'

Mike's mouth was moving but no words came out. My heart slowed to a regular rhythm as I waited. I knew in that instant that whatever Mike said, I would not change my mind. I could choose the life I wanted. I watched a smile spread across his face. 'So are you going to accept his proposal?'

'Not yet. I want to carry on working on the agoraphobia. I know Jim wants to look after me, and in a way that's lovely, but I don't want him to have to be my nurse. You could transfer me to a Devon service, although I would rather travel down once a month to see you.'

Mike stood up, so I did too. 'Miss Jenny Drake, may I be the first to congratulate you on making a splendid decision! I am absolutely delighted for you both,' and with that he formally shook my hand.

All I could say was, 'Do you mind if we finish the session, or at least have a break? I need to ring Jim. He might want to know my plans.'

Mike laughed as he turned round and reached for his phone. 'Use nine to dial out, while I go and make us some coffee to give you some space.'

I simply waved my brand new mobile phone in his direction, and he laughed and left the room.

So that is how I came to make a rather romantic phone call from a very untidy office, smoothing dust off a half-dead plant, as I explained my next move to my overjoyed soulmate.

As I spoke to Jim, I knew that at last my life was taking off. My heart began to soar.

I humbly thank:

Penny, for inspiration.
Steph and Merrilyn, for gently suggesting changes.
Ken, for quietly cooking when I was away in a fictional world.